MUSE

A Kate Redman Mystery: Book 15

Celina Grace

Muse
Copyright © 2023 by Celina Grace All rights reserved.
First Edition: April 2023

No part of this book may be reproduced, scanned, or distributed in any printed or electronic form without permission. Please do not participate in or encourage piracy of copyrighted materials in violation of the author's rights. Thank you for respecting the hard work of this author.

This is a work of fiction. Names, characters, places, and incidents either are the product of the author's imagination or are used fictitiously, and any resemblance to locales, events, business establishments, or actual persons—living or dead—is entirely coincidental.

The Kate Redman Mystery Series

In chronological order

Hushabye
Requiem
Imago
Snarl
Chimera
Joy (a short story)
Echo
Creed
Sanctuary
Valentine (a novella)
Siren
Pulse
Descent (a novella)
Fury
Tasteful (a novella)
Scimitar
Performance
Hunt
Muse

For my son, Jethro, my top G
With all my love

Author's Note

In Muse, Kate refers to an earlier case where several severed human feet were found in and around Abbeyford. That case is based on a real-life event that took place in the city of Bath in the UK (whilst I was actually living there!).

My fictional interpretation of that case is found in the novella, Tasteful, which also has more than a little bearing on the events of Muse...

Prologue

THE NAKED WOMAN LAY SPRAWLED on the wooden floor. Her head was turned to one side, one cheek mashed against the hard boards. Her eyes stared ahead. Hair fanned out from her head in a thick auburn spray, one tendril drooping over her forehead. It fell over her squashed cheek and trailed in the dust on the floor. Her arm was twisted awkwardly, elbow and palm pointing upwards, her fingers splayed.

Mae Denton put down her pencil for a moment and flexed her own fingers. She'd been sketching in total concentration for at least ten minutes, and her hand was cramping. Not to mention that her pencil point had been worn down to a nub. Looking critically at her life portrait so far, she regarded the model lying on the floor. *Poor woman*. Not only must she be uncomfortable, but she must also be very cold... Mae could see gooseflesh on her own arms, and a cold draft crept around her ankles, so God knew what the model must be feeling.

"They *do* get paid well," her friend Lucy had said,

when Mae had pointed this out to her in an earlier class. "In fact, I've even thought of having a go."

Mae had laughed. "Not in front of Johnny and Kai, you wouldn't.

"Oh, wouldn't I? Give me thirty quid and I'll strip off here and now for *you*."

Smiling at the memory, Mae sharpened her pencil, although she could see by the clock that the class had only a few minutes left to run. The curtains to the classroom had not yet been drawn and the windows showed an uncompromising blackness. It was mid-January and darkness fell early.

"All right, everyone, time's up for today. Please gather everything you need and return anything to the cupboards that doesn't belong to you."

Mr Barker took the evening life drawing class, as well as several of the lectures during the week. There was an unkind rumour going around the college that he did so because he was an old perv, but Mae thought this was probably untrue. There *had* been a few teachers at the Abbeyford College of Art and Design whom she would not have fancied being trapped in a classroom with alone. Mr Neville for example, who'd left under something of a cloud last year, not to mention that psycho who'd killed those girls, or persuaded them to kill themselves, all those years ago. That had been well before Mae's time at the college but, of course, something like that was always going to pass into gruesome legend. Still, she reminded herself, at least they weren't *all* like that...

The model had got off the floor, rather stiffly, enveloping herself in a grubby beige dressing gown. She was in conversation with Mr Barker, rubbing at the arm she'd been lying on. Mae looked again at her sketch, not best pleased with what she'd done. Still, there was always next week. They tended to have the same model for a month at a time and they were only a fortnight into drawing this particular one.

Johnny caught her eye from across the room and winked. He mimed lifting a pint to his mouth and raised his eyebrows.

Mae shook her head with some regret. A session in the Green Man after a class was always fun – she knew Lucy would be there with Anna and Taya and Kai – but tonight she had an appointment to keep.

She mouthed back, *I can't* and shrugged.

"Why not?" asked Johnny, as he caught up with her at the door.

"I've got to—" She stopped herself saying *meet someone*. It would only lead to questions. "I've got to be somewhere."

"Where?"

"Never you mind. It's not important." They were outside now, with the others, everyone calling goodbye and heading for the car park or the footpath that led back to Abbeyford town. The life drawing classroom was on the very edge of the campus. "Are you going to the pub?"

"Yeah, course. Why don't you sack off this mysterious appointment and come?"

Mae looked up at his handsome face, his dark hair drawn back into a bun on the top of his head. He was so tall she had to tilt her face right back. "I really can't. But I'll be as quick as I can. I'll try and meet you guys there."

"Want me to walk you there – wherever there is?"

"No, I'm fine. You go on. I'll see you later."

Johnny hesitated, but her tone was firm. "All right. See ya later, alligator."

Mae watched him walk off in the direction of town. It was a shame; he was so cute, but he just wasn't her type – even considering, well, her situation as it was... Hot on the heels of that thought came the other, that made her look at her phone and begin to hurry off down the other path, the one that led to the quarry.

She was twenty yards down the path when something in the woods to the side rustled, a twig snapping. Mae pulled herself up, her heart thumping. She was using the torch on her phone to light her way and she swung it towards the direction of the sound. A pair of eyes flashed red in the torchlight and Mae gasped, before realising that it was a deer, just a deer. The animal turned and crashed away through the dead bracken, its white rump glowing briefly in the light before disappearing in the darkness.

Ruefully, Mae shook her head. She wasn't that jumpy normally, but these woods could be spooky, especially at night. She caught sight of her phone screen before the backlight dimmed and faded and saw the time. Better hurry... She walked on, quickly, her boots scuffling through the fallen leaves.

Behind her, hidden by blackness, the person who'd been following her stepped out from the edges of the woodland. As Mae began to walk again, they moved quietly after her, treading almost without sound, following the girl as she walked further and further into the night, further into the darkness.

PART ONE

Chapter One

"I'M GUESSING YOU'RE DOING DRY January this year then, Kate?"

DI Kate Redman had just walked into the lobby of the Abbeyford police station, where PC Paul Boulton was manning the desk. Somebody had forgotten to take down a length of Christmas tinsel from the top of the computer monitor. It twinkled through the safety glass that, ostensibly, protected the officers on reception from both Covid and any recalcitrant customers they were booking in.

"What?"

"Dry January. I guess you have to do it anyway?"

"What are you talking about?" Belatedly, Kate clocked what he meant. "Oh. Ha ha. Yes, I suppose I am." She hadn't spared Dry January a thought, given the other things on her mind at the moment.

Paul's gaze fell to her belly. "Oh, well, I suppose you've got other things on your mind at the moment."

"You can say that again. By the way, that tinsel needs to come down, it's bad luck after the twelfth."

Winking at him as he rolled his eyes and reached

for the tinsel, she let herself in the door that led to the offices on one floor and the cells and interview rooms on another. Kate would normally have taken the stairs – the main office was only two flights up – but at six and a half months pregnant, she thought she'd earned the right to take the lift.

The office was busy. For once, most of the usual crowd were there; not on leave, out interviewing or escaping to the pub or canteen. Kate waddled across to her desk and subsided, with a sigh of relief, in her chair.

DS Chloe Wapping, who sat opposite her, gave her a wave of greeting. "Bird, you're fatter than ever."

"Gee, thanks. How to lift a girl's spirits in one short sentence."

"You surely don't have much longer to go."

"Afraid so. A few more months yet. Well, it all depends really."

DS Theo Marsh bounded up to the two women. "Kate, mate. How's it going?"

"Well—"

"You look like you're having twins!"

Kate rolled her eyes. He said this every day and it never got any less annoying. "I *am* having twins, you idiot."

Theo giggled. "I know, I know. Want a coffee? Oh no, right, you can't have one. *What* a shame. Mwahahaha."

Kate raised a stapler threateningly. "Would you

bugger off? Get me a herbal tea if you actually want to do something useful."

Chloe grinned at her from across the table. "Bet you're going to miss this, right?"

"Huh." Kate returned the stapler to her desk and turned her attention to her computer. "Right, what have we got? Is Mark going to debrief?"

She looked across to the office of DCI Mark Olbeck, her old friend and colleague (and boss) but, as usual, he had his phone headset on and was busy talking and typing at the same time.

"Think so. There's that fraud case that keeps coming unstuck."

"Oh, God, that one. It's like a bad smell that keeps hanging around."

"I know—" The rest of Chloe's remark was interrupted by the ringing of her desk phone. She picked it up and answered in the standard manner.

Kate turned her attention back to her screen. She looked at her list of emails, groaned inwardly and then clicked on the icon for her calendar. She looked at the dates a month from today. Would she still be working then? Was it possible that she might actually be a *mother* by then? It seemed incredible. Seven and a half months – no, that was too early. Far too early for comfort. She patted the mound of her belly. "Hang in there, guys," she murmured, under her breath. It still, even now, seemed incredible enough that she was pregnant, let alone pregnant with *twins*.

She remembered the scan, the first one, twelve weeks along. She and Anderton had waited nervously in the hospital waiting room, women in varying degrees of bulginess surrounding them. Kate had had terrible morning sickness for the first six weeks, bad enough to take some sick leave from work, but at three months, it was finally abating, thank God. Perhaps that should have been a clue, but she and Anderton had still had the shock of their lives when the flickering images on the sonography machine had shown two little trembling hearts.

Afterwards, Anderton had said "All I heard after that was a massive rush of blood going to my head. It literally *fizzed*." Kate had said nothing but had gasped and turned to her partner with a smile that had a touch of mania about it.

"Do you want to know the sex?" the sonographer had asked and they'd both said "No!" in unison. As Anderton had said to Kate in the car on the way there, "There are so few real surprises in life, aren't there? But this is one of them."

Well, more fool them because there was that other, double surprise waiting for them. Kate had almost got used to the idea now and she was actually glad, very glad, because she knew that this pregnancy was probably her last shot at becoming a mother. A little gremlin that hadn't popped up for a while now whispered in her ear *You already are a mother, aren't you, really, don't you remember your teens?* and she set her teeth and mentally swatted it away.

"Kate?"

Kate came back to reality to realise that Chloe was waving at her. "What?"

"Just had a call from the front desk. Another girl's been reported missing."

Kate sat up. "Oh, really?"

No fewer than three girls, all late teens or early twenties, had been reported missing in the past two years. Despite extensive investigations, none had yet been found, alive or dead. Kate recalled the missing women; Hannah Treeble, Saskia Devonshire and Prisha Kumar. Not to mention the Bristol girl, Poppy Taige, who had disappeared a few years ago and had also never been found.

"Her parents reported her missing. She went to a late art class last night, at the art college and never came home."

Normally, missing people would be dealt with by the uniformed officers. Because of the multiple cases still not solved, it had been passed to their department to investigate. Kate thought back to what had happened before when the calls had come in.

"You took the Devonshire case, didn't you Chloe? I mean, you did first contact with the relatives and so forth?"

"Yeah. Me and Martin. Rav and Theo were on the others though."

"Right." Kate thought about looking through the files but decided against it. After a moment's thought, she heaved herself out of her chair and went to Olbeck's office.

"Mark?" At least he was no longer on the phone. He waved her inside.

"You're looking very well. Blooming."

"Blooming fat," said Kate, grinning. "But thanks."

"What's up? We've got debrief in twenty minutes."

"That might be sooner once you hear. Another girl's gone missing."

Olbeck looked concerned. "Oh no."

"Yes. Another young one, a student at the art college."

"Right." Olbeck tapped his fingers against the top of his desk. "God, not another one. Right, Kate, find out what you can before we all meet. You can speak to the others about it."

"Do you want me to take it on?" Ordinarily, this would be below Kate's paygrade but given the seriousness of the situation, she felt like she should offer.

Olbeck pondered. "Actually, you know, yes, I would. We need experienced hands on this." Then he smiled. "Unless you think you might not be around here for much longer to see it through."

Kate groaned. "I don't want to tempt fate. But it's fine. I'll take it on."

"Good woman."

They said goodbye and Kate returned to her desk,

sitting down again thankfully. Each day this pregnancy brought a brand-new sensation, if not actual pain, then definite discomfort.

The name of the most recent missing girl was Mae Denton. Kate read through the scant notes that the front desk had taken. The girl's parents had reported her missing when she failed to come home last night, from a late-night art class at the Abbeyford College of Art and Design. Kate knew it fairly well. Her brother Jay had gone there, years ago now, and there had been that awful case with the suicides and – what was that other one? – oh yes, the death threats received by several women, including a student at the college. Shaking her head at the depravity of humankind (not for the first time), Kate looked up the address details for the Dentons and began to gather her things together.

Chapter Two

NORMALLY, THE ABBEYFORD OFFICERS WORKED in pairs, particularly if their destination or interviewees were known to be suspicious or even downright dangerous. This time, nothing warranted pulling another officer away from their work – Kate could easily deal with this on her own.

It was a beautiful winter day, the skeletal trees outlined against the low golden sunlight slanting down through the scudding clouds. The ground glittered with frost. All very picturesque, thought Kate, as long as you could observe it from a warm car or house. The twins would be born in the spring and Kate was glad. She remembered her sister-in-law telling her the best time to have a young baby was in the summer. "If you're going to be up and down all night, at least it's not freezing cold," Laura had said. Kate was due in April, but she knew well enough that very few first babies arrive on schedule. As she pondered, one of the twins shifted within her and kicked her painfully in the bladder. "Easy, guys," she murmured, patting her belly once more.

Perhaps they could have a little dinner party before the twins arrived, she mused. Just a few guests. Olbeck and Jeff, Chloe and Carl. Maybe Rav and Jarina but they'd recently had another baby so would probably decline. And Theo and DCI Weaver, newly married – *Nic, Kate, Nic, how many times?*

As she entered Arbuthon Green, the suburb in which the Dentons lived, Kate reminisced about Theo's wedding. It *had* been rather fun. The couple had hired a barn for the reception. They'd had a hog roast and a country and western band, which given Theo's usual taste in music was absolutely hilarious, but it had been a hoot. Kate, being rather too pregnant for much dancing, had sat it out on the hay bales that were dotted around the barn, holding her lemonade and cheering on Anderton, Martin and Rav who were do-si-do-ing with the best of them.

Arbuthon Green had come up in the world since Kate had moved to Abbeyford. Once one of the most insalubrious areas of the town, it had slowly gentrified over the years and now rivalled neighbouring Charlock for the most affluent, middle-class suburb in the area. The Denton's house was a three-story sixties townhouse – not Kate's favourite period of architecture – but she could see it was well maintained, the gravel driveway in front neat and weed-free, a potted bay tree by the front door.

Kate parked and heaved herself out of the car. She was barely halfway to the door when it opened and a woman who had to be Mae Denton's mother looked out. Her face was drawn with anxiety, her dark hair pulled back into a careless bun.

"Are you – are you from the police?"

"That's right. Are you Mrs Denton?" Kate showed her warrant card as the woman nodded and opened the door to admit her.

Kate was ushered into the sitting room, a bright, open-plan space with the kitchen at the back. A modular sofa looked comfortable, and Kate subsided onto it trying to stifle a groan of relief. There was a man in the room, seated opposite her and at once he got up, his hand outstretched.

"I'm Steven Denton, Mae's father. I can't tell you how worried we are, this is so out of character for her, she never does anything like this—"

Kate interrupted him as gently as she could. "I'm sorry, Mr Denton, I can appreciate it must be terribly worrying for you and your wife. If I can just take down some details, we can get started on trying to find her as quickly as we can."

"Yes – yes of course." He sat back down abruptly, looking near tears.

Mrs Denton came into the room. She was almost wringing her hands. "Could I – would you like a cup of tea?"

Kate marvelled at the instinct of the British – even in the direst circumstances, a hot beverage would be offered. It was heart-warming, in a way. "No, no thank you, Mrs Denton."

Mae's mother perched herself on the sofa next to her husband. "We – Mae's not – she's not a wild one, not really. She isn't *thoughtless*. She'd never stay out all night and not tell us, not ever."

"Yes, I see." Kate gently took the parents though the standard questions. Mae was nineteen, studying Fine Art at the Abbeyford College of Art and Design. She didn't have a boyfriend (privately, Kate thought *that you know of*, but of course, she said nothing). Her best friends were Lucy Atkins and Johnny Papmier. Kate noted these names down – they would both have to be spoken to.

"It sounds so obvious, but I presume you've tried ringing her?" Kate asked, eventually.

"Of course we have." Tears were trembling on the edge of Mrs Denton's eyelids. "That was the first thing we did. It just keeps going to voicemail. I've left her no end of messages."

"And you've tried her friends?"

This time it was Mr Denton who spoke up. "We've got Lucy's number, that's it. I tried – I tried to find the others through Facebook, but they don't seem to have – I mean, I couldn't find them."

"Does Mae have Facebook? What about Instagram?"

One of the tears escaped and tracked its way down Mrs Denton's face. "Yes – yes, she had both. Do you think I should try messaging her friends on Instagram? I don't really know how it works..."

Neither did Kate, if she was honest, but she said nothing of the sort. "I really would attempt to reach her friends on any kind of social media platform you can. We'll be contacting the college to get their contact details, which we can pass onto you with their consent." She smiled as reassuringly as she could. "I know it's very difficult, but please do try not to worry. The chances are Mae will be home very soon."

But would she, though? Kate doubted herself, even as a couple of uniformed officers arrived at the house to stay with the parents, and Kate could say goodbye. There had been too many girls go missing recently. Kate eased herself into the driver's seat. Time to adjust it again, although there was only so much space to be had before she couldn't actually reach the pedals. One of the twins kicked and wriggled as she attempted to get comfortable. Boy, it was an odd sensation... Chloe had asked her more than once what it was like, and Kate had, uncharacteristically, been lost for words. Like having an alien inside you, she'd said once, and Chloe had grimaced in horror.

As Kate drove away, she thought about that, the innate strangeness of growing another person – or in this case, two other people – inside your own body. "Wait until they're born," her oldest friend Hannah had told her, herself a mother to three. "There's nothing that prepares you for the total mind-melt of actually seeing your own face in someone else's."

Kate rubbed her stomach. "Settle down, you guys." How odd to think that there would soon be two new people in the world, all being well. All being well... Kate didn't dare to think that thought. *I can't lose them. Stop it, woman, stop it. They're fine and healthy and all will be well.*

Once the search for Mae had been set in motion and the case taken on, Kate handed her notes over to Chloe and sat in with Olbeck to brief him. She was eager to get home, to put her feet up and talk to Anderton, if he were home. He'd been so busy lately and she knew it was because he was trying to bring in as much money as he could before the babies arrived. She loved him for it, but it meant that they hadn't had much time together, just the two of them. They really should make the most of it whilst they still could.

She drove home in a blaze of winter sunlight, the pavements glittering as if rimed with tiny diamonds. The house was empty and silent when she pushed open the front door. Kate sighed. An added pang came when she remembered Merlin, her beloved cat, as likely as not would have come to greet her as she came into the house. No more. Three months ago, Kate had come downstairs in the morning to find him lying in front of the cold woodburning stove, equally as cold. He had been an old cat, she knew that, and she'd been prepared, as much as you could ever be prepared but, oh my word, the pain... He'd lived a lovely long life with her but still, she'd wept and wept, tears dropping onto his dulled fur as she stroked his head over and over again. Even Anderton, coming downstairs after her, had had to clear his throat a couple of times.

One of the babies kicked her, startling her out of her melancholy. One of them clearly had their foot in her bladder as well, again. Thank goodness for a downstairs loo. Kate took care of business and then went into the kitchen. She could see the little Acer maple tree that marked Merlin's grave at the end of the garden, its branches bare now. When they'd planted it in the autumn, the leaves had been almost startlingly scarlet. *Poor old cat*. Why don't you just get another, Theo had suggested, when she'd been particularly mopey at work one day. He didn't understand. Perhaps only pet owners would understand...

Sniffing a little, Kate regarded the contents of the freezer. She'd become a much better cook over the past few months, to Anderton's delight, but tonight, it would be something very simple indeed. She didn't have the energy for anything more elaborate than something on toast. In fact, even that was too much for her at the moment. Kate waddled into the living room and lay down on the sofa. Five minutes rest, that was all... She turned on her side, cupping her belly with both hands, and drifted off to sleep.

Chapter Three

THE MORNING PAPERS HAD BEEN delivered by the time Kate and Anderton had come down to breakfast – unusually early for once. The fine weather had departed, and the day was grey and blustering, the odd squall of rain freckling the kitchen windows as Kate made toast and filled the kettle with water. She allowed herself one coffee a day and it was particularly welcome that morning.

Two newspapers were waiting on the table for her perusal – *The Times* and the semi-local paper which covered news across Somerset and Avon. Kate reached for the nearest, the *West Country Comet*.

"I feel we might be the last people in the country to actually have a paper newspaper delivered," she remarked to Anderton, who was busy slapping marmalade on his toast.

"Well, perhaps. Comes in useful for fire lighting, though, doesn't it?"

"Mmm." Kate took a sip of coffee, unfolded the paper and scanned the headlines. Britain sending weapons to Ukraine; a Conservative minister engulfed in a sex scandal; graffiti artist Banksy's latest work selling for an unprecedented sum... Nothing very gripping. She turned the front page over and choked.

"What is it?"

Kate didn't answer him for a moment. She was too busy reading the headline on the second page – *Local Police Baffled by Mystery of Missing Girls* – and taking in the by-line of the journalist who had written it. *By Tin Johnson*.

Tin. After all these years. Kate had once been virtually engaged to him. They'd parted fairly acrimoniously, but there hadn't been anything to tie them together – no children, no shared assets, no mutual friends, even. She hadn't thought of him in years. Last time she'd heard or seen of him – how? Facebook perhaps? – he'd married and was living in New York.

"What is it?" Anderton repeated. Kate ignored him, her eyes running down the lines of print.

Anderton growled and grabbed the paper from her.

"Oi!"

"What's all this? Who's this? Oh, it's him, isn't it, young Tin." Anderton scanned the page. "What's he doing back here anyway? Didn't you say he was in America?"

"He was," Kate said, faintly. It wasn't that she regretted breaking up with Tin – and it *was* years in the past – but still, it was a bit... "Bit of a blast from the past."

"I'll say." Anderton turned the front page and began to read the following one. "And I'm not sure in your case I'd be so happy to read this, to be honest."

"Let me see." Kate reached for the paper and Anderton let her have it. "What's he saying?" She read for a moment and set her lips. "Ah. The usual. How we're making a complete mess of the investigation. Hah. As usual."

"It's clickbait, Kate, it's some crappy little paper. No one cares."

"Hmm."

"Didn't you say he was working for the *New York Times* or something? If I remember that far back."

"God, I don't know. I stopped following his career years ago." Kate started re-reading the article from the start. Some of the phrasing made her wince, particularly as, well, Tin did actually have a point. Why weren't they further ahead with the investigations? Put in black and white, *literally* in black and white with the paper and ink, why had so many young women disappeared without trace over the past few years? She finished the article once more and stared ahead of herself.

"Kate?"

Kate pulled herself back to the present. One of the twins shifted within her, waking up his or her brother or sister, who began something that felt like a womb aerobic workout. Kate winced.

"Kate? You okay?"

Kate rubbed her belly. "I'm okay. Juniors are getting lively."

"It's that coffee, I keep telling you. Why don't you have herbal tea or something in the morning?"

"Because it's the *morning*. I'd never get out the door otherwise."

"You know best," said Anderton, diplomatically. "Anyway, forget that stupid article. I'll line Merlin's litterbox with it." There was a moment when they both winced. "Oh, no. Sorry. I'll chuck it in the wood-burner."

"No, it's okay." Kate folded it up and put it to one side. "Right, I have to go. I'm not sure when I'll be back tonight."

"Okay, well, give me a call."

He gave her a kiss and then patted her stomach. "Bye, you lot."

The rain had intensified, and Kate switched on the windscreen wipers as she drove away from the house. She thought about the article and, by association, Tin. How many years had it *been*? She knew she'd read about him being married somewhere, before she'd decided not to waste any more mental energy obsessing over Ex-boyfriends. That brought Dr Andrew Stanton to her mind, although that was such ancient history that she could almost forget they'd once dated. He and his wife had come to one of the Halloween parties she'd had before. Hadn't that party been where Chloe had met her boyfriend, Roman, the one who'd died so tragically in the London attacks of a few years ago? Kate sighed. What a bloody few years it had been, what a strange and traumatic few years... The pandemic was barely over but already it was receding into the past, the lockdowns and the hospital admissions and the government announcements taking on the air of something that had once been a strange dream...

"Do you remember us washing down our shopping?" Kate asked Chloe when she got to the office.

"What?" Her friend looked at her with quirked eyebrows.

"During lockdown. The first lockdown. People were actually washing down their shopping with disinfectant. Or quarantining it for a couple of weeks."

Chloe shook her head, as if marvelling. "I know. It seems mad, now."

"But we didn't *know*, did we? We didn't know how it was passed on." The two of them sat quietly for a moment. "Madness now, of course, but isn't everything in hindsight?"

"Yes." Chloe typed a few lines and looked up again. "Boy, I bet you're glad you're pregnant now and not then."

"You're not wrong."

"Can you imagine how *awful* it would be to be a first-time parent in lockdown?"

The words 'first-time' gave Kate a moment's pause. She and Chloe had never talked about what had happened to Kate in her past – the adoption of her baby. Of course they hadn't, because Chloe didn't even know. Unless someone like Olbeck had enlightened her – but no, he would never do that, he respected people's privacy.

Kate became aware that Chloe was waiting for an answer. "Oh, yes. Awful. So isolating."

Chloe looked sombre. "You know, I think we're only just starting to see the long-term effects of lock down, to be honest. I really do."

"The long-term effects?"

"Yes. The psychological effects, the impact it had on people's mental health. That sort of thing. And what about the children? They missed out on *two years* of school, essentially. That can't be good."

"I'm sure you're right." With an effort, Kate pulled her mind back to the job. She would need to visit the Dentons again, chase up the college for whatever information they could give her, organise a search of the surrounding woods and grounds, arrange for information boards to be put up, interview all of Mae's close friends... Trouble was, she didn't feel like doing any of it. Instead she felt like going home, climbing into her comfortable bed and going to sleep, for about, ooh, a hundred years...

"Kate?"

"Sorry." Kate pushed her hands through her hair, shorter now and shaped around her face. "Just thinking of everything we have to do."

Chloe gave her a wry look. "Bird, you can delegate, you know. What's most important?"

Kate gave herself a mental shake. "Yes, you're right. You're right. Come over here and let's start going through the list."

Chapter Four

THE SEARCH FOR THE MISSING girl was organised for the next day. Normally, Kate would have been right there with the searchers, scouring the ground, sweeping the woods and forests for something, anything that might lead them to Mae Denton. Now, her delicate condition meant she could remain in the office, watching the search on the TV that hung from the ceiling, as journalists from both local and national news channels reported on what was happening.

Rav and Chloe were the only others apart from Kate in the office. Rav brought Kate over a cup of herbal tea without asking. Kate thanked him.

"You're welcome."

Kate gave him a glance. "My God, Rav, you could pack clothes into the bags under your eyes."

"Gee, thanks. I've got a new-born baby, remember?"

"How is she?"

Rav yawned. "Up all night. Then Ali gets up at six o'clock and doesn't stop. I tell you, I come to work for a rest." He looked at her stomach and smiled. "And you've got all this to look forward to. Double the fun!"

"Oh, ha ha." Kate was too fat to be able to slap him from where she was sitting but she raised an arm threateningly and he dodged, giggling.

Kate had gone back to the Denton's house the day before, although her second interview with Mae's parents had yielded very little more than her first. As far as her parents were aware, Mae had no boyfriend. They had managed to contact all of Mae's friends, although as by now her disappearance was front page news, they had all known anyway. Neither Lucy Atkins or Johnny Papmier had any idea what had happened to their friend – or so they said. Johnny Papmier was the last to have spoken to Mae and Kate had already sent Martin out to interview him more thoroughly.

Would the search find anything? One part of Kate hoped that it would, even if it meant finding the girl's body. At least then they would *know*, there would be closure. Her parents would have a body to bury and a grave at which to mourn. How much worse would it be to not know what had happened to your darling child? Or would there be the slightest bit of comfort in not knowing, in being able to tell yourself that they were still alive, somewhere, just unable to make their way home?

She should really go back to speak again with the Dentons but a craven part of her didn't want to. She sat there for a moment, both hands cradling her bump. The twins were quiet underneath her hands. Chloe's words reoccurred to her. *Bird, you can delegate, you know*. Kate knew she was pretty bad at that and to be honest, it was something that she needed to get to grips with sooner rather than later, given that she was going to be on maternity leave at some point.

She cleared her throat. "Chloe, would you mind taking on the Dentons for me today? They may find it easier to talk to you and if not, a fresh face might help. They'll need support as much as anything."

Chloe looked up. "Yeah, sure. No problem. Shall I go now?"

"If you can."

Chloe nodded. She packed up her stuff and pulled on her heavy tweed coat. Kate turned her attention back to the TV for a moment, but the coverage of the search had finished and some sort of cookery program had succeeded it. Kate reached for the remote and turned it off.

Chloe strode towards the door and slowed. She swung around to face Kate. "Kate—"

"Yes?"

Chloe looked almost awkward. "Do we have any suspicions regarding the parents?"

Kate wasn't shocked. She knew, as well as anyone, that many crimes are committed by someone known to the victim. "Not as yet. Obviously, we're keeping an open mind."

Chloe nodded. "I'll see you later then." Then she added, in a tone of surprise, "God, it's snowing."

Kate looked out of the window. Sure enough, tiny

white flakes were spiralling down from the sky. "So it is."

Chloe said what every British person said on first sight of snow. "Of course, it probably won't settle."

"Probably not. Cold for them out on the search."

Chloe shivered theatrically. "Just be glad you can stay here in the warm. I'll catch you later, bird."

"Bye."

Kate scooted her wheely chair over to the window. As she watched, Chloe emerged from the front door of the station and scurried towards the car park, head bowed against the thickening snow. It *was* settling. Tiny drifts were starting to pile up on car windscreens and in the corner of the window frame. Despite being in the warm, Kate found herself shivering.

"I wonder how they're going out there," she murmured to herself, thinking of the searchers out in the woods.

The snow was falling hard by now. Theo cursed the fact that he'd left his gloves – his warm, wool-lined leather gloves – back at home. Nic had given him a cashmere scarf for Christmas and at least he'd remembered that this morning, thank God. He tugged it tighter around his neck.

He was supervising one group of volunteers, assisted by PC Dai Williams. They'd already covered much of the ground either side of the footpath that led away from the college, the last place Mae Denton had been seen. Nothing had been found, other than the usual detritus; discarded gloves (none suitable for purloining, thought Theo), empty vapes, crisp packets and other rubbish.

"God, it's brass monkeys out here," panted Dai, crashing through the undergrowth towards Theo. "I can't even feel my hands."

"Me either, mate." Theo demonstrated the fact by shoving them under his armpits in a futile attempt to warm them. "Any luck?"

"Nothing so far."

Theo looked ahead, to where the path dipped out of sight, down a hill. "The quarry's down there, isn't it?"

"That's right."

"Who owns it? National Trust?"

Dai shook his head. "No, no, it's council, as far as I'm aware."

As it happened, Theo knew the area quite well. When he'd been in college (not the art college, just the sixth form one attached to his school), the quarry had been one of the places to hang out, especially in summer. Bonfires were of course strictly forbidden, but that hadn't stopped Theo or any of his school mates from building them. Looking back from an adult perspective, it was something of a wonder they hadn't burnt the forest down.

The search advanced slowly. After forty minutes or so, they reached the edge of the quarry. Rough-hewn steps had been cut into the sandstone walls, leading in a slow spiral to the quarry floor. The ground was uneven, although softened by undergrowth and drifts of sandy soil. This was heathland, thought Theo and remembered those long-ago college days, when the boys would sometimes pretend they'd seen an adder, in the mostly futile hope of sending the girls into a panic...

Dai began to direct the other searchers to spread out across the quarry floor. Theo walked forward himself, gaze sweeping from side to side. There was more rubbish here, but old rubbish; weathered and grey. The whole of the scene was like a sepia photograph, faded and brown, beginning to be overlaid in a faint white blanket of snow.

Except for one thing. Theo's sharp eyes spotted something over by the far wall, a pinprick of bright pink, incongruous against the beige background. Quickly, he walked over towards the little spot of colour lying on the sandy floor and bent over it. A fingernail, a fake fingernail, candy-coloured and hard as a beetle's shell, lying on the ground by a faded tuft of heather. Theo held his breath, reaching for an evidence bag and his tweezers. He thought he could see a trace of blood at the edge of the nail, a blackened rim against the cheerful pink. He took a photograph of it with his phone and then carefully manoeuvred it into the bag, sealing it tight. He held it up against the dying sunlight, the curve of it black against the light, like a small, ironic grin.

Chapter Five

"So," said Olbeck, the next morning. "I'm sure you're all aware that the search for Mae Denton turned up a fingernail. A fake one, an acrylic one – are they made out of acrylic?" He looked over at Chloe and Kate with his eyebrows raised.

"Don't ask *me*," said Chloe. "I think I last painted my fingernails in about 2002."

"Same here," said Kate.

"Well, anyway, it's been sent off to the labs for a 24-hour turnaround. The nail did have some remnants of a human nail attached to it – as if it had been ripped off." He saw Kate wince. "I know, not very nice. But as we all know, a fingernail is not a body. Nor do we yet know if it even belonged to Mae."

Chloe raised her hand. "I'm back with her parents today, guv. I'll check if they can confirm whether she had those kinds of nails on when she went missing."

Olbeck nodded. "Anyone got anything to suggest?"

"Yeah," said Theo. "I've been thinking about this. We need to go in hard on her friends – harder than we have. You know what kids that age are like, they know things about their friends that the parents don't."

"I agree." Olbeck indicated the list of names on the whiteboard. "Mae's circle of friends. You can parcel them out between you but make sure they are all reinterviewed as a matter of urgency."

"I'll take the girls," said Theo with a grin.

Olbeck shot him a look. "Of course you would, Theo. You're a married man now, remember?"

"Ah, I'm only joking…"

Olbeck smiled. "So am I. Yes, take the girls. Chloe, can you and Kate take a guy each, as it were?"

Chloe stifled a giggle. "Yeah, sure."

Olbeck looked at Kate. "Kate, you okay with that?" After a moment's silence, he asked again. "Kate?"

Kate looked up. "What?"

"Are you okay with interviewing one of Mae Denton's friends?"

"What? Oh, yes, yes, sure. Sorry." Kate stifled a yawn. It was embarrassing, but she'd been moments away from sleep, right there in her office chair.

Olbeck favoured her with a sympathetic glance. "Why not take Johnny Papmier? He lives not far from you, then you can head straight home afterwards."

"I'm all right," said Kate, slightly annoyed. She knew he was being kind, but it felt a little patronising. "I'm not on maternity leave yet."

"Fair play, mate, you are growing two extra human beings," said Theo. "That's got to take it out of you."

"Yeah," chipped in Rav. "I mean, I'm knackered with Isla, okay, but at least I'm not recovering from gestating and giving birth to a whole new person."

Kate held her hands up in surrender. "*Okay*. Thanks for the support, guys, but I'm really fine. Honestly." Even as she said it, she could feel how tempting it would be to head straight home after interviewing the witness... head home, climb the stairs and fall onto her deep, deep, soft bed...

She blinked herself awake again and tried to concentrate. Olbeck was taking them through their other cases but naturally, Mae Denton's disappearance had top billing. Kate forced herself to make notes, just vague scribbles, but having to move the pen nib over the paper in her notebook at least kept her from falling asleep again.

Back at their desk, Chloe peered at her anxiously. "You really do look a bit knackered, bird. Why don't you do what Mark suggests and go home for a rest after your interview?"

Kate was fed up with trying to appear normal. Theo was right. She was pregnant with twins, for God's sake, she deserved to put her feet up for a bit. "Okay, okay, I will. But I'll interview Johnny Whatsit first. Is he Mae's boyfriend?"

"No, I don't think so. Just a good friend, apparently. Here, here's the file we have so far."

Kate took the slim folder from Chloe with thanks. She remained standing – she wasn't sure that if she sat down, she'd be able to get up again in any good time. Johnny Papmier had already been interviewed once, briefly, as he was apparently the last person to have spoken to Mae Denton before her disappearance. Kate raised her eyebrows.

"Has someone run a background check on Papmier yet?"

Chloe shrugged. "If they have, it should be there."

There was nothing relevant in the folder. Tutting, Kate sat down and fired up the various databases she needed, inputting Papmier's name and searching for any previous convictions, cautions or anything else that could prove relevant.

"Anything?" asked Chloe, after a few minutes.

"Not that I can see. Oh, wait—" Kate homed in on a portion of the screen. "There's something – oh, just a caution. Remember when those students chucked that statue into the docks in Bristol?"

"The slave trader one?"

"That's the one. Well, apparently, he was part of that crowd. Along with several hundred others."

Chloe came around to Kate's desk to have a look for herself. "Not exactly much to go on, really."

"No, indeed." Kate finished her investigation of the records held and exited the program. "Well, I'll head off and interview him." She glanced at the clock. "And then, you know, I might actually head home."

Chloe gave her a one-armed hug across the shoulders. "Do that. Seriously, you don't want to take any risks with these little ones."

"No," agreed Kate.

"Can I touch your bump?"

Kate grinned. "Yes – and thank you for asking. You wouldn't believe the amount of people who just lunge for it without even so much as a by your leave." One of Anderton's friends – admittedly quite drunk at a dinner party – had actually fallen to his knees in front of her and *kissed her stomach*. Bloody weirdo.

Chloe gently rubbed Kate's protruding middle. "So weird. You don't expect it to be so – hard." One of the twins moved beneath her fingers and she snatched her hand back with a shriek that made Rav and Theo look up from their desks. "God!"

Kate couldn't quite double over with laughter, but she gave it her best shot. "Your face…"

Chloe was laughing herself by now. "Sorry. You can't deny it feels really weird, though."

"How do you think *I* feel with that going on inside me?" Still giggling, Kate patted Chloe on the arm. "Anyway, I'll see you later."

"Tomorrow," warned Chloe.

"Yes, sorry. Tomorrow."

Chapter Six

KATE HAD CALLED JOHNNY PAPMIER's mobile and spoken to him, arranging to meet him at his home after he'd finished college for the day. He'd sounded wary, but not antagonistic. He lived in Charlock, the suburb next to Kate's own and, like most of his contemporaries, still lived at home with his parents.

She found his house without difficulty, knowing the area quite well. It was a 1950s red brick, semi-detached with the front garden paved over in concrete to allow two cars to park there. Kate compressed her lips. Yes, parking was a perennial issue in Abbeyford but paving over front gardens was disastrous environmentally. Another little patch of habitat gone and another little patch of impervious concrete to add to the flooding next time there was heavy rain...

Anyway, this wasn't why she was there. Kate ran a hand through her hair, settling it around her face, and retrieved her warrant card from her bag. As she waited for the door to be answered, she glanced about, ascertaining the type of family who might live here. It wasn't a particularly attractive house – in fact,

Kate would bet that it was actually ex-council – but it was solid and sturdily built. Rather sterile – there were no flowerpots, or shrubs or anything green on the concreted front garden. Despite the paving, there were no cars parked there at the moment.

Johnny Papmier opened the door himself. He was very tall, well over six foot, and towered over Kate. A good-looking young man, dark hair pulled back into a knot at the back of his head, heavy black eyebrows and dark brown eyes. Kate held up her card and introduced herself.

"Uh, yeah. Come on in."

Kate thanked him and made her way inside. The hallway was poky, laminate on the floor resembling grey wooden floorboards. A bundle of coats enveloped the post at the bottom of the staircase. Johnny directed her into the living room, a space both cluttered and homely. Kate chose the single armchair, leaving Johnny with the sofa.

"Thanks for seeing me, Mr Papmier." She smiled at him, hoping to put him at his ease. "Is it okay if I call you Johnny?"

"Uh – yeah. Sure." He sat down on the sofa, looking awkward.

Sometimes at this point, Kate would request a hot drink or a glass of water, in order to have a sneaky look around the room. But she could see, even from a swift glance, that this room belonged to Johnny's parents. There was a knitting basket tucked beside the sofa, a *Daily Mail* on the coffee table before her and the general impression of lives that were comfortable, serene and perhaps a little bit boring.

Kate had given up wondering why young people were still living at home in such droves. The state of the housing market told you everything you needed to know. She silently thanked God or the Universe or whatever deity wanted her gratitude, that she'd been able to buy her first flat years ago, when you didn't need to be a Russian oligarch to be able to afford even a modest home.

Johnny appeared to remember his manners. "Um, would you like a cup of coffee or something?"

"No, I'm fine thanks." Kate clicked her pen in a brisk manner. "Now, I understand that you're good friends with Mae Denton?"

"Um. Yeah."

"More than friends?"

Johnny frowned. "What do you mean?"

Kate would have thought it was obvious what she meant, but she clarified her statement. "Are you romantically involved with her?"

An indefinable emotion crossed Johnny's handsome face. "Uh, no. No, we're just mates."

Kate thought back to the interviews already undertaken with Mae's female friends, Lucy Atkins and Anna Evans. Both had said that they thought Johnny had been 'keen' on Mae, but the feeling hadn't apparently been reciprocated. "Would you have liked to have been her boyfriend?"

"No," Johnny said, just a shade too quickly. He seemed to realise this and hurried on, "I mean, yeah, she's pretty fit, so yeah, I fancied her. A bit. Everyone does, really. But nothing happened – I mean, we were just mates. Good mates."

"I see." Kate made a few notes on her notepad, more for the look of things than anything. "I understand you were the last person to see her before she disappeared?"

A frown stitched Johnny's black brows together. "Well, the last person but one, don't you think?"

Kate looked up. "What do you mean by that?"

"I mean – well – the guy that – that got her." He looked away suddenly, blinking. "*He* must have been the last person to see her."

Kate was silent for a moment. "Do you think that's what's happened? Mae's been – abducted?"

Johnny looked back at her, full in the face. She could see tears in his eyes. "Well, don't you? I mean, come on, man, all those girls going missing... Mae's just the latest. I don't understand..." He trailed off as his voice thickened.

"I can see that you're very worried about her," said Kate, after a moment. "Did she ever talk to you about someone in her life that she was scared of, or threatened by? Anything unusual like that?"

Johnny swiped a large hand under his nose. He

wore a ring around his middle finger that looked as though it were made from twisted silver paper, although Kate could see that it was solid metal. "No, nothing like that. She wasn't *scared* of anyone."

"Had she mentioned wanting to go away for a bit, go on holiday, leave Abbeyford for whatever reason?"

Johnny looked scornful. "What, run away? That wasn't Mae's style. Anyway, she was happy, she didn't have any worries that I knew of."

Kate was also of the opinion that Mae Denton wasn't a runaway, but she kept that to herself. A couple of the missing girls had been from 'troubled' backgrounds and at least one of them was a habitual runaway. Which one was it? Kate clawed around in her head for the name – Hannah Treeble, that was who. She'd been reported missing several times by her foster parents before she disappeared for good. One day Hannah just hadn't come back.

She brought herself back to the present. "Did she ever give you the impression that she was hiding something? Or someone?"

For the first time since they'd started talking, Kate could sense a reserve in Johnny Papmier. It was almost too faint to put a finger on but her interviewing skills were finely honed. She pressed him. "Anything at all?"

Johnny looked down at the carpet. "Well – there was – I mean, sometimes she wouldn't exactly be open about what she was doing. Kind of, not cagey, exactly, but it was like she didn't want to tell you."

"Tell you what?"

"Oh, you know – tell you where she was going, who she was meeting, that kind of thing?"

Kate made notes. "Did this happen often?"

Johnny shrugged. "Well, kind of. Like the last time – that last night – I just asked if she was coming down the pub—"

Kate remembered this from the first interview. "That would be the Green Man, right?"

"Yeah. I work there part-time, just a couple of shifts a week." This was news to Kate, and she jotted it down. Might be worth talking to the management at the pub, see if they could shed any further light on the group dynamics if Mae and her friends were frequent visitors. She turned her attention back to Johnny, who was still speaking.

"So, she just said she couldn't – I mean, she said she had to be somewhere—"

"But she didn't say where?"

"No. Just gave me a smile and headed off." He stopped talking and turned his head away, blinking.

Kate pondered. She had the impression that Johnny wasn't telling her all he knew, but was he keeping back something about Mae's last words to him, or was it something else? Did he actually know who Mae had been going to meet – or whatever she had left to do – or was he telling the truth and the faint reticence was to do with something else?

Out loud she said, "I appreciate what you're saying,

Johnny. Can I just take you back over the last time you saw her again, step by step?"

It was dark by the time she left his house, and a cold wind was gusting, rain thrown in spatters over the windscreen as she drove away. The twins had been quiet while she was interviewing, but the rumble of the car engine obviously woke them up as they began to twist and dive about within her. One managed to get their foot lodged under her rib cage, which was so uncomfortable she had to pull the car over, get out and begin a ridiculous series of twists and manipulations to try and release it. The absurdity of what she must look like by the side of the road made her laugh. Finally, the tiny foot freed, she wedged herself back into the driver's seat and drove home.

Chapter Seven

ANDERTON WAS WATCHING THE NEWS when she got in. The wood-burner was alight, and the curtains drawn in the living room against the night. Save for the gaping hole left by Merlin's continued absence, everything was cosy.

"Hello you."

Kate bent to kiss him, with difficulty. "Hi, love." As she straightened up, sighing a little, she caught sight of the television. The search for Mae Denton was being reported on once more.

Anderton saw where she was looking. "It's third on the bill. Pretty big story now."

Kate sat down, sighing again. "Well, beautiful young girl, gone missing. Beautiful young *white* girl, gone missing no less. Respectable, middle-class family. No trace of her except a fingernail. Got everything the media needs, hasn't it?"

"Sadly, yes." Anderton heaved himself up off the sofa. "How are you feeling? Babies been playing you up?"

"No more than normal." Kate eased a hand to her back and rubbed it.

"I'll get you something to eat. Put your feet up."

Kate did as she was bid as Anderton headed to the kitchen. Not for the first time, she gave thanks for a supportive partner. Of course, it helped that he'd done this all before (a long time ago now, to be fair) and – perhaps more importantly – he was determined to be a better father this time around.

As she was, to be a mother. She'd been thinking of that time in her teens more and more frequently. Kate knew it was no doubt a normal response to her situation, but it was – unsettling. Years of therapy had meant she thought she'd packed the guilt away, but perhaps that was impossible. She'd packed it down instead – but it seemed it was always there, ready to resurface.

She shook herself mentally, determined to dispel these gloomy thoughts. As if they'd read her mind, both twins appeared to wake up and began moving, slow little wriggles at first, but clearly gearing up for a fine evening of acrobatics. Kate smiled, despite the discomfort. Perhaps the babies really could sense her mood, through her bloodstream, her hormones, the very brain that was involved in keeping them alive and healthy. She remembered a sign she'd once made for herself, years ago now, to hang by the mirror that stood by the front door of her old flat. *Thoughts become reality. Choose good thoughts.*

That sign was long gone but it was good advice. Kate rested her hands on the swelling curve of her belly, hoping the warmth would sooth and comfort the twins into restfulness again. She leant her head back against the back of the sofa and closed her eyes. In the background, she could hear the news presenter move onto the next story. For now, Mae Denton's disappearance was off the air. Kate sighed yet again, wondering whether the next report would be the discovery of the poor girl's body. Would that be worse for the family? Of course it would be terrible, the total rupture of their world – but would it be worse to have no body at all? For ever and ever... Kate thought of the Moors murderers, those awful crimes in the sixties and the heartbreak of the poor mother who was never able to lay her son to rest. The evil of it, the depravity.... Kate held her belly once more, this time protectively. When Anderton came back, with a steaming plate of food, she was fast asleep.

The next day dawned cold and frosty, but bright, the low winter sun sparkling on the whitened grass and plants of the garden. Kate, who'd managed to wake herself to eat some dinner, had slept well. She said as much to Anderton.

"That's good. They obviously like sausage and mash."

"Indeed."

"What are you up to today?"

Kate paused. She no longer discussed her cases in

any detail with Anderton. It was no longer appropriate. At one time, this would have been awkward, but his consulting business was now so successful that his long tenure as a police officer was comfortably in the past.

It was easy to stick to generalities. "More interviewing. I want to go back through some of the earlier disappearances too."

"Good idea." Anderton checked his watch and bent to kiss her. "Right, I'm off. Got a meeting."

"See you," said Kate, yawning. She remained at the table, watching the sunlight gradually strengthen, falling in golden stripes across the glittering lawn. If Merlin was still alive, he would have jumped into her lap – or tried to, Kate not having much of a lap left at the moment. She closed her eyes against the jab of pain. "I miss you," she said, out loud. She thought of something she'd read, not that long ago, about people who'd seen their beloved pets after death – a glimpse out of the corner of their eye, the sound of their footsteps on the floor. She would give almost anything for that to happen, thought Kate. She wouldn't even be scared. She even stayed at the table for a moment longer, straining her ears, but of course there was nothing. She put a hand to her belly and rose, feeling a little bit ridiculous.

Sunny it may have been, but it was still gaspingly cold. Kate turned the car heater up to full while she scraped away at the windscreen, removing the overnight frost. On her way into the station, she changed her mind, heading straight for the city centre. Why not go straight to the Green Man and check with the management as to Johnny Papmier's employment? Normally it would be too early in the morning for the pub to be open, but since the pandemic she'd noticed that a lot of pubs were opening earlier, for coffee and breakfast meetings, no doubt to try and make up the profits lost during Covid times.

She was able to get a parking space in the small car park of the Green Man, something else that happened when you arrived early. Kate had already had her one real coffee of the day at breakfast, but the warm, chocolatey smell that greeted her nostrils as she walked into the pub meant she decided, guiltily, to have just one more. A small one.

The Green Man ran a successful quiz on Tuesday nights and, when the demands of the job allowed it, Kate and her teammates joined in. With the combined intellects of herself, Chloe, Rav, Theo and Martin, they often did quite well and had once won the coveted £50 bar tab as first prize. That had been quite a messy night, Kate remembered with a grin. It made a small cappuccino look respectable.

Or so she thought, until she ordered one at the bar.

"That'll be a decaff, right?" asked the bar girl, her eyes on Kate's bump.

"No, a normal one," said Kate, trying to sound

breezy. The girl looked at her as if she wasn't fooling anyone.

Oh well, made what she had to do easier. Kate pulled out her warrant card – the girl's eyes widened – and asked to speak to the manager.

Chapter Eight

"So, have you heard?"

Theo came bounding over to Kate as soon as she set foot in the office. For once, he didn't mention the fact that she was having twins, so Kate realised it must be something fairly important.

"No, what? I've literally just got in; in case you haven't noticed."

"The fingernail I found. Turns out it's a DNA match to Mae Denton."

Kate felt a hollow pang in the region of her stomach and, for once, it wasn't because of the babies. "Oh," was all she said.

"Yeah, I know. Mark's going to debrief us in a moment. Want a coffee?"

Kate waited for the punchline of glee that she couldn't have one, but nothing came. Theo *must* be worried. "Oh – thanks. I can't though."

"Yeah, right, right. I'll get you a tea."

Kate thanked him and waddled to her chair. Chloe looked up as she sat down. "You've heard."

"Yes."

Chloe shook her head. "I mean, we were fairly certain but it's different when it's a certainty, isn't it?"

"Yes." Kate felt that more effort was needed. "I mean – Mark *did* point out that a fingernail is not a body. I mean—"

"Yeah, I know. But..."

"But," agreed Kate. She switched on her monitor and waited for it to warm up. "Still, let's see what he says."

She'd barely read the top two emails in her inbox before Olbeck was commandeering the floor. He didn't waste any time with preamble.

"Now, I guess you've all heard the news that the fingernail found in Oxley Quarry is indeed Mae Denton's. DNA samples from her home match completely." There was a brief murmur around the office. "Yes, I know, it's not a great sign. But let's have your thoughts on it before we proceed. I also want to know anything else that might have happened during your investigations."

Theo raised his hand. "Well, that nail was ripped off, there was blood at the base of it. Suggests an altercation, something violent, doesn't it?"

"But there was no blood found at the scene," Martin said. "I know that doesn't mean that nothing happened, but—"

"Yeah, well – isn't the most likely explanation the most obvious? She's been abducted, almost certainly by a man."

There was something tickling at Kate's memory, something about the fingernail. What was it? She frowned, trying to will the memory to the front of her mind but it resisted.

Olbeck continued. "Now, as I'm sure you're aware, abduction is a likely scenario but it's not the only possibility. It may be that Mae has simply run away. It's not an uncommon occurrence in teenage girls, after all." He fell silent for a moment. Kate wondered whether he was thinking about his own daughter. But, given as Poppy was a mere three-year-old, he had some time to come to terms with the possibility.

Chloe raised her hand. "I've been going through the old files on the other girls who've disappeared." Kate shot her an approving look but as Chloe was looking at Olbeck, it wasn't acknowledged. "One of them in particular, Hannah Treeble, was a habitual run away."

Rav protested. "There's nothing in any of the interviews with Mae's family or friends that she had a troubled domestic life. Her parents – well, they just wouldn't accept that possibility that she'd run away. Why would she need to? That's what her dad said to me, literally the last time I interviewed them."

Chloe gave him an annoyed glance. "Well, if they had anything to do with it, they would say that, wouldn't they?"

"But—" began Rav before Olbeck, ever the peacemaker, raised his hands for calm.

"It's a possibility," he said. "*Yes*, Rav, we can't discount it completely – but, as it happens, I agree with you. It seems unlikely. But it stays on the board." He put his words to actions, scribbling up 'abduction?' 'runaway?' on the whiteboard behind him.

It was Theo's turn to raise his hand. "I did a bit of a deep dive on some of the scum we've had up for similar offences. The ones on release and all that."

"Similar offences?"

"Yeah, you know, abduction, sexual assault, stalking. All that lovely stuff." Theo's mouth quirked up at the corner. "Thought I might see if there was a particular MO, or pattern that might have come up."

Olbeck looked pleased. "Good work, Theo. Good use of initiative. Was there anything?"

"Er – no." Theo's look was so crestfallen that Kate bit back a giggle. Poor Theo, he'd been trying... She knew he was hoping for a promotion soon. In fact, she wouldn't put it past him to make a grab at her job, while she was on maternity leave, the cocky little bugger. But right now, she couldn't get too worked up about it.

Martin spoke up. "I did have a theory," he said, rather hesitantly. Martin was the quietest member of their team – not shy but reserved. His very reserve made his rare suggestions ones to listen to.

Olbeck looked interested. "Yes?"

"Well..." Martin hesitated again. "It sounds far-fetched, I know, but – what if she wanted to disappear? I don't mean as in a runaway sense, more that she wanted to walk out of her own life."

There was silence whilst everyone digested this somewhat startling theory.

"Can you elaborate?" Olbeck said, cautiously.

"Well, I mean, it's been known before, hasn't it? Faking your own death – or if not your actual death, leading people to believe that it's a possibility." Martin looked around at the circle of sceptical faces and half-laughed. "I'm not saying that's definitely what's happened. It just occurred to me, that's all. I mean, how hard would it be to break off a nail and leave it at the scene where you were last known to be heading?"

There was another silence. Then Theo spoke up.

"He's right you know. Like that bloke, that MP, in the sixties. Snowhouse. No, Stonehouse. Faked his own death, left his clothes on a beach and disappeared."

Kate knew who he meant. ITV had screened an absorbing drama about the story not that long ago.

"Well..." Olbeck didn't look convinced. "I'm not saying it doesn't happen. I just think it's not something that teenage girls are known for."

"No, I know," agreed Martin, not easily embarrassed. "It's just – it did occur to me, so I thought I'd bring it up."

"Fair enough." Olbeck paused as something else occurred to him. "Sorry Martin, but doesn't the UK have something like a quarter of the world's CCTV cameras, or something daft like that? If Mae had taken herself off, why haven't we seen her on any of the footage that we've viewed?"

"Is it really that many?" asked Chloe, looking fascinated.

"Well, don't quote me on that. But yes, the UK has a *lot* of CCTV."

Kate, conscious of the fact that she'd contributed precisely nothing to this debrief, tried to cudgel her brain into thinking of something. There had been something, just now, she'd tried to remember something – what was it? She cursed her increasingly terrible memory.

Olbeck was talking, assigning them all tasks and advising on the investigation going forward. Kate was distracted by the pair of shoes he was wearing, some rather natty tan brogues. A new pair? She blinked, trying to focus. Just then, the memory she'd tried to retrieve came crashing back into her mind, and she sat up with what was almost a shriek.

Everyone turned to her in enquiry.

"Got something to add, Kate?" Olbeck asked, smiling at her.

"Yes! Yes, sorry, it just occurred to me. Remember those feet that we found, years ago?"

"Feet?" Olbeck looked puzzled and then his face cleared. "Oh, yes, *those* feet. The art exhibit, wasn't it? God, how long ago was that?"

"Years," said Kate, trying to find a more comfortable sitting position. "It's probably nothing at all but something about this just reminded me."

"In what way?"

"Well—" Now that she was articulating her thoughts, Kate was beginning to think it was a rather stupid idea. "Well, it was just the idea of body parts, in the countryside. That was all. It just reminded me. What with the art college involved and all." She could feel the well-meaning interest of her colleagues shading into something like indulgence. *Pander to the pregnant lady, don't get her upset...* Such paranoia, Kate, she told herself, as she finished, rather lamely. "Well, it just occurred to me. That's all. It's probably nothing."

Olbeck gave her a kind smile. "Well, like everything, it goes up on the board." He turned and wrote up a succinct summation of what Kate had just said. "Right. Incidentally, I think some more interviews with the students and staff at the college might be a good idea. Anyone want to take that on?"

"I will," said Kate, partly as penance for her ridiculous suggestion.

"Thanks, Kate. Come and give me the rundown later."

Chapter Nine

It was another cold, crisp sunny day, rather pleasant, as long as you weren't stuck outside for too long. Kate drove to the college, squinting against the sunlight. She realised, as she found a parking space, that she hadn't let Olbeck know about her interview with the manager of the Green Man. Not that there was much to tell. Harry, the manager, hadn't been able to tell her much about Johnny. He'd only worked there for a few months and was on a zero-hours contract, so his hours of work at the pub varied wildly.

Bright as it might be, the feeble warmth of the sunrays hadn't yet melted the frost on the grounds of the college. The shortcuts across the lawns made by generations of students were frozen into ruts and dips of solid mud, rimed with frost. Kate picked her way carefully over the icy footpaths to the reception area.

It had changed a little since her brother Jay had come here – unsurprisingly, really. With a qualm, Kate realised her little brother must be well past thirty. In fact, it was his Thirty-second birthday coming up next month. She made a mental note to get something in the post (and hoped she'd remember it).

The reception area had been extended from the poky hallway that had once stood here. Now it was a bright, glass-roofed area, with comfortable sofas placed against the walls. The artwork on the walls was, naturally, from the various students – and very good it was too, thought Kate, peering closer at the artist signatures. She was a little shocked to see that one picture, a small, charming study of a woodland glade, was signed by Mae Denton. That made her look closer. There was something faintly familiar about the painting, but Kate couldn't put her finger on what it was.

There was a cough behind her, and she turned to find the Deputy Head of the college facing her, a woman she knew vaguely through previous dealings with the college. Deirdre Something – no, Deborah, was it? Luckily, the woman was wearing a lanyard and a quick downward flick of the eyes showed that Kate was right with her second guess. Deborah Coombes.

"Detective Inspector?"

"That's right." Kate proffered a handshake and showed her card with the other hand. "Thanks for seeing me."

"I suppose you want to talk about Mae." Deborah Coombes looked anxious. "Is there any news?"

"Nothing new, I'm afraid. I wonder, could we speak somewhere privately?" Kate gestured to her stomach with a smile. "Could do with sitting down, to be honest."

"Oh, of course! Of course. Do come this way."

Kate was ushered to a pleasant office at the back of the main building, looking out on the courtyard that served as the main social meeting place of the college – at least when the weather was less inclement. Today, only a few hardy students could be seen over by the far wall, next to the entrance that led to the grounds. White clouds of exhaled breath or vape smoke rose from their huddle.

Deborah Coombes seated herself behind her desk and Kate sank thankfully into a chair, facing her.

"Yes, as I said, unfortunately there is no news on Mae's disappearance. What I wanted to talk to you about was her friendships – her relationships with the students here – and her relationships with her tutors, if you can help me with that?"

"Yes. I see." Deborah looked troubled. "Well, I didn't exactly know Mae, not personally. I knew of her, of course."

"I see she contributed a painting to the reception area."

Deborah raised her eyebrows. "Did she? I'm sorry, I don't know—"

"It's fine." Kate thought it wasn't important. "Who would you have said were her closest friends?" She knew this already but wanted to see what the woman told her.

"Oh. Well – I suppose it would be Lucy, Lucy Atkins. And I suppose, Anna Evans. The three of them seemed very pally."

"Yes," said Kate, pretending to write this down.

"And Johnny Papmier, I'm not sure if they were a couple or not, but they certainly did spend a lot of time together."

"Yes," said Kate again, trying not to sigh audibly.

"And Geraint Winner, she was spending quite a lot of time with him lately."

Kate's head snapped up. "Geraint Winner?"

Deborah smiled, apparently unaware of having given Kate some fresh information. "Yes, he's a first-year drama student. I saw Mae with him quite a few times, here and there. She gave him a scarf."

"Sorry?"

"Mae gave him a scarf. They were out in the courtyard, just the two of them, and I saw her take it off her neck and give it to him. He was laughing. He's quite a quiet lad, quite withdrawn, so I remember it as I was quite pleased to see he'd made a friend."

Geraint Winner. Why had this name never come up before? Not in interviews with Mae's parents, or her friends? Kate, mind working busily, hid her excitement. She asked for details on Geraint Winner; his contact number, his address and his tutors, which Deborah Coombes gave to her willingly and with seemingly little curiosity.

Much as Kate wanted to chase up this new lead,

she had an appointment with Mae's art teacher to keep. She found Mark Gregory in one of the studios in the new arts block, an airy, white-painted building with a lot of skylights and floor to ceiling windows. He was just dismissing a class and Kate stood back from the doorway as a stream of teenagers flooded out talking and laughing.

"Mr Gregory?" He looked up apprehensively. Kate smiled at him. "DI Kate Redman. We spoke on the phone?"

The teacher seemed to relax. "Oh, yes. Hello Inspector. I would say it's lovely to meet you but that seems, well, somewhat inappropriate given the circumstances."

"Yes." As Kate entered the room, his gaze inevitably fell on her bump. It was funny, annoying as the attention could be, she would kind of miss it when it was gone. The twins were quiet for now, gentle, lazy stirrings all that she could feel.

"Let me get you a seat." Mark Gregory pulled one of the folding wooden chairs forward. "Not too comfortable, I'm afraid, but it's better than a beanbag."

Kate smiled politely as she tried to sit down gracefully. "I'd like to talk to you about Mae Denton, Mr Gregory."

A spasm of something crossed his face. She had the impression he was mentally squaring his shoulders. "Yes. Poor Mae." He leant forward a little. "Is there – is there any news?"

Kate gave him the same words she'd given to Deborah Coombes. "I'm sorry," she added.

Gregory seemed to shrink a little. "I didn't expect there to be but – well, there's always hope, isn't there?" For a moment, real pain was visible on his face.

"You were fond of Mae?" Kate asked.

He looked startled, startled and a little annoyed. "*Fond*? Well – that's not exactly the word I'd use – I suppose – well, I liked her. She was an excellent student."

"Can you tell me more about her, Mr Gregory?"

"Call me Mark, please. Even the students call me Mark." He smiled a little. "We're pretty informal here, DI Redman."

Kate didn't encourage him to drop her title. In her opinion, a little reserve always came in handy. "Thanks, Mark. Anything you can tell me about Mae would be useful. What she was like as a student – you said she was excellent – did you mean academically?"

"Well, yes, there was that. She did some very accomplished work."

"I saw a picture of hers in the reception," said Kate.

"Oh yes. The quarry. That was a nice p—"

"The quarry?" Kate couldn't help but interrupt. "That's a painting of the quarry?"

Mark looked faintly surprised. "Yes. Oxley Quarry."

Kate reminded herself that the finding of the fingernail and its match to Mae was not yet common knowledge (although no doubt the media would be reporting on it very shortly). "You know that was apparently where she was heading when she disappeared?"

"Was she?" Mark Gregory said, blandly. "I'm not sure I knew that."

Kate hesitated, just for a second. Surely *that* knowledge was in the public domain? Did it matter?

Gregory spoke again. "I'm sorry, Inspector but I deliberately haven't followed any of the news on – on this. I find it very - very distressing." He blinked and looked away, another spasm of pain evident on his pleasant, blunt-featured face.

Kate could understand that, and said so. "Can you tell me about Mae's relationships with her friends? Particularly Lucy and Johnny?"

She listened and noted down what he told her, nothing earth-shaking or that she hadn't heard before. Lucy was apparently 'quite a live-wire' and Johnny 'cleverer than he looks'. Mae had been 'a sweet girl, really sweet. That came out in her work, a sort of gentleness, a fluidity...' Kate nodded and fought not to roll her eyes.

Eventually, Mark Gregory wound to a halt and Kate looked up. "What about Geraint Winner?" she asked.

Gregory looked puzzled. "Who?"

"Geraint Winner. He's a first-year drama student here."

"Oh. Oh, yes, I have just about heard of him. Unusual name, isn't it? I don't teach him. I'm afraid I know almost nothing about him."

"Are you aware that Mae and he appeared to be friends?"

Gregory frowned. "Um, not that I was aware. But, honestly Inspector, I don't keep tabs on my students like that. Mae was perfectly free to be friends with whoever she wanted." He hesitated, as if about to say more, but settled for giving Kate a warm but dismissive smile.

Walking back towards the reception area after her meeting with Mark Gregory, Kate paused for a moment before Mae's painting on the wall. The quarry, her teacher had said. Kate peered closer. It didn't look *much* like the quarry, from the photographs she had seen, but perhaps it was an impressionist work, or the painting had been done from a different viewpoint. Kate glanced behind her at the quiet reception area and dialled Geraint Winner's mobile number. It rang through to voicemail and she left one, stating her name and rank and asking to see him. When she got back to the office, she'd send an email too. Kate paused once more, reading the little white sticker at the base of the framed painting, noting for the first time the name of the painting. *Secret Place, Mae Denton, Watercolour* and the date. Kate took a quick snap of both painting and label, and then made her ponderous way back to her car.

Chapter Ten

When Kate got back to the office, the sun had disappeared behind a blanket of thick, grey cloud. Although the days were gradually lengthening, darkness still fell far too early for Kate's liking. *Come on Spring, get a move on...* She locked the car and made her way through the front entrance of the station, if only because it was a shorter walk to the lifts than going in the side entrance.

She raised a hand to PC Dai Williams who was staffing the reception desk. Despite the plastic partitions, he was also wearing a navy-blue facemask. It looked odd now, even this close to the end of the pandemic. *How quickly we forget*, thought Kate, pressing the button for the lift. She remembered going shopping with Olbeck during the height of the Covid years, in one of the breaks between lockdowns. They'd gone to the garden centre and Olbeck had forgotten his mask, so Kate had nipped in and bought him a pack from beside the till, taking it back outside for him to don. How they'd laughed when they realised she'd brought the child size ones...

Repressing a chuckle at the memory of Olbeck buying compost with a tiny pink polka-dotted mask on his face, Kate hit the button for the second floor. As luck would have it, Olbeck was just coming out of the office as Kate stepped out of the lift, and she told him what she'd just remembered.

He laughed, before looking sombre. "Actually, you know, I've been thinking about that."

"What, shopping for compost?"

"No, you numpty. I meant the pandemic."

Kate paused. "What do you mean?"

For a moment, Olbeck looked as though he was going to say something else but decided against it. "Never mind, it'll keep. How did you get on at the college?" As Kate began to tell him, he grimaced and checked his watch. "Hell, sorry darling, I've got to go. Meetings."

"Obviously."

Olbeck squeezed her arm and made for the lift. Then he turned back. "Actually, you free later? For a catch up?"

"Workwise?"

"Well, not really. Just feel like I should make the most of you actually being able to go out for the evening. Fancy a drink and a bite to eat?"

Kate thought quickly. Actually, she had pregnancy yoga that evening, but any excuse to miss that... "I'd love to," she said. "Anderton too?"

"Why not? God, I've got to go. See you later."

Kate blew him a kiss as the lift doors closed upon him.

Because she knew she'd forget otherwise, she texted Anderton the night's plans as soon as she sat down. Chloe was absent, but Rav came over once she'd settled herself.

"Did you go to the college?"

Kate nodded, filling him in on what she'd learned. "I left a message for this Geraint, but there's nothing yet."

"I can chase him up for you, if you like? I know you're busy."

"Thanks, that *would* be good. I mean, it's probably nothing but it's a name and a contact we haven't heard of before, so it needs looking into."

Rav sat himself down in Chloe's empty chair and leant forward over the desks. "Seems a bit strange that none of her friends mentioned him."

"Mmm." Kate shifted in her seat, trying to get comfortable. "Maybe they just didn't know they were friends."

"But that's weird, isn't it? Like, especially with Lucy – she's Mae's best buddy, isn't she?"

"Yes." Kate pondered. "Yes, that is a little strange that none of them ever even mentioned him."

Rav sat back with a sigh. "She – Mae, I mean – is still front-page news. All over social media."

"I can imagine."

"All sorts of mad theories flying about."

"Of course." Something occurred to Kate in a moment of panic. "Oh, God, please tell me the quarry is still cordoned off?"

Rav crimped his mouth for a moment and then relaxed. "Yeah. Yeah, it is, it will be until we hear otherwise."

"Thank God for that. Imagine all the Tik-Tokers and YouTubers up there, trying to get selfies and film themselves playing detective."

"Trampling all the evidence..."

"Exactly," said Kate and they exchanged an eloquent glance.

Rav sighed once more and then pushed himself upright. "We've had all the nut-nuts in the country ringing up, of course. Claiming they've spotted Mae, or have her trapped in a dungeon, or something like that."

"Well, that's par for the course. As long as they're being followed up." Kate added. "And I'm not sure we should be using the term 'nut-nuts'."

Rav waved his hand in a very Theo-like manner. "Pfft. Anyway, I'll get onto what's-his-name for you."

"Ta."

By the time Kate was ready to leave, Anderton had texted to say he'd meet her and Olbeck at the Black Cat wine bar, and to get a bottle of their best red on tab. She swung by Olbeck's office to collect him and she drove them both there, knowing that she wouldn't be drinking anyway.

They secured their favourite table at the back, right by the woodburning stove, glowing coals within it giving off a welcome heat. The venue had recently changed their menu and Kate and Olbeck perused it while they waited for Anderton.

"This all looks delicious," said Kate, "But given that my stomach is now the size of a walnut, I feel I may just have an entrée."

Olbeck patted her knee. "Not long to go now."

"A few months yet, dude." Mentally, Kate added, *please God.*

"Are you going to have any help? You know, a nanny or something?"

Kate sipped her lemonade. "I'm not sure. I suppose – well, no, I know it would help."

"How does Anderton feel about it?"

"Feel about what?" Anderton loomed up at the table. Olbeck sprang up with a cry of welcome and a hug (he had always been a hugger – Kate knew that Anderton was almost used to it by now). Kate held up her face for a kiss, having no intention of getting out of her chair.

They sat and chatted about children and babies and mother's helps – "Sexist," said Kate and Anderton laughed and said he'd be needing a *father's* help more than she would – until their food arrived. Kate nibbled cautiously at some salt and pepper squid, trying not to envy the men for their huge plates of ribs, chips and vegetables gleaming with butter.

As the level of food on their plates diminished, conversation resumed. Kate remembered what Olbeck had said to her in the corridor at work that day and reminded him.

"What's that?"

"You know. You were talking about the pandemic."

"Oh yes—" began Olbeck before Anderton interrupted with a groan.

"Dear God, wasn't living through it bad enough? Do we have to keep talking about it as well?"

"But that's the thing!" Olbeck swung around in his chair to face Anderton who was sitting by his right. "That's the point. We *aren't* talking about it, not really."

Anderton frowned. Kate said nothing but kept listening.

Olbeck continued. "I don't mean in the papers and on the TV and all that. Although—" He paused for a moment, thinking. "Although thinking about it, there hasn't exactly been a flood of films or programs yet, has there?"

The three of them pondered. "Perhaps it's a bit soon," suggested Kate. "It might be seen as, well, insensitive, to be creating entertainment out of something still, well, raw."

"That's true." Anderton was nodding. "Remember 9/11? Took years for Hollywood to start addressing that, didn't it?"

"I can't remember," said Kate. "But I imagine that

not many people want to relive lockdown, even in fictional form."

"That's it," said Olbeck. "But the point is, the point I'm making, is that nobody is talking about it in real life."

"We're talking about it now," Kate pointed out.

He gave her a look. "Yes, all right, clever clogs. I'm saying collectively people aren't really talking about it." He was silent for a moment and then added, "It's a bit 'don't mention the war', isn't it?"

The three of them contemplated that thought for a few moments.

"You're right," said Anderton. "Which is weird, really, isn't it? We've all gone through this massive collective trauma and now we – what, we're supposed to pretend it never really happened?"

There was another moment of silence.

"It's very British," said Kate.

"I don't think it's just *that*," Olbeck pointed out. "The whole world went through it."

"Hmm."

Kate felt that there was more to be said, that there was more she wanted to say, but she couldn't think what. Perhaps that was the problem. The whole thing was, at the moment, too big to put into words.

One of the twins stirred within her and instinctively she went to cover her bump. At least it's over now, she thought. I'm not bringing them into a pandemic, not anymore. *There but for the grace of God...*

She said nothing though, not even to Anderton, and the three adults carried on silently looking into the flames of the wood-burner.

Chapter Eleven

KATE SPENT THE NEXT MORNING in the office doing some digging. This was probably the most tedious part of her job, but unfortunately, it was also the part of her job most likely to yield results. She made a list of all the witnesses she'd spoken to over the past few days, and began to methodically research them, prioritising the ones who were closer to Mae Denton personally, or who had had more contact with her over the last year.

Both the office manager of the college and Mark Gregory had sent over Mae's college reports at Kate's request. Reading through them, Kate could see that Mae had been a conscientious student, if not a brilliant one. Her undoubted talent lay in her painting skills as opposed to her academic work, which was routinely marked in what Kate thought of as a 'good effort but not actually that great' way. Practical projects, such as the quarry painting and several still lives were highly graded. Socially, Mae appeared to be a well-liked member of her classes, with very little disciplinary action ever needed – a mere matter of occasional lateness and once, tardiness in handing in an assignment.

Kate got up for a stretch of her legs and to make a cup of cranberry and rose-petal tea. As she waited for the tea to steep, she wondered why herbal teas were often so disappointing. A lovely big whiff of scent as you first poured in the hot water and then – well – very little flavour in the cup. After hearing Kate complain about this at some length, Chloe had tracked down a rare make of herbal infusions, which at least meant that Kate felt she was drinking *something*. Making a note to thank her friend, again, for helping out, Kate took her steaming cup back to her desk.

"Is that one of mine?" Chloe asked as Kate sat down opposite her. Kate confirmed that it was and reiterated her thanks. "Cool. What's happening this morning?"

Just as Kate opened her mouth to answer, her phone rang. She and Chloe exchanged a 'what are you going to do' glance before Kate answered it.

"DI Redman? It's Mark here, Mark Gregory."

Kate sat up a little and reached for her pen. "How can I help you, Mr Gregory?"

"It's probably nothing." That phrase was guaranteed to make Kate sit up a little further again, even with the hesitation in his voice. Kate encouraged him to speak. "Well, I remembered today – I'm so sorry I didn't say yesterday but I'd honestly forgotten and, I don't know, I really don't know if it's relevant—"

"Please do go on, Mr Gregory."

"Right. Yes. Well, it's just that Mae and Johnny, you know, Johnny Papmier did some work experience last year, at one of the galleries in Salterton. You know, by the sea."

Kate did know Salterton. "Yes?"

Mark Gregory sounded even more hesitant. "Well, like I said, it's probably nothing. I mean, it literally was only a two-week placement with the gallery, we do it every year, not just with that gallery."

Kate thought she could vaguely remember one of Mae's friends mentioning something about an art gallery but, as usual, the name of who it was had escaped her. She made a quick note on her writing pad to look it up. "Go on, please, Mr Gregory."

This time he didn't ask her to call him Mark. "Yes, sorry. The gallery – it's called Sea Views by the way – it was the first – no, sorry, second time we'd placed students there. No problems before, nothing that anyone had said."

"But there were problems this time?"

Again, Gregory hesitated. "Well, I wouldn't say *problems*. Not exactly… It's just Mae told me that she didn't like the owner. Thought he was a bit of a creep."

"Right." Kate made more notes. "Anything in particular she mentioned? I mean, did he – I'm assuming it's a 'he' – actually assault her or harass her?"

Gregory sounded shocked. "Oh no, nothing like that. Well, I don't think so. I feel sure she would have told me..." He trailed off for a moment. "Anyway, she just said to me, erm, one day after class, that she found him a bit of a creep. A bit, you know, letchy."

Gregory sounded almost embarrassed, but Kate could understand it. Her opinion of Mae rose slightly – telling a male teacher about sexual harassment could not have been easy. "Can you tell me in any more detail?"

"I'm sorry – that's literally all she said. I did try and get her to explain a bit more, but she was – well, understandably reluctant."

"I see. What happened then?"

"How do you mean?"

"I mean, did you contact the gallery owner, or anything like that?"

There was a pause at the end of the line. "I did think about it." Mark Gregory sounded troubled. "But Mae was adamant that she didn't want any fuss. And it was the end of the placement, and no more students were going to be sent there that year, so, well, I sort of forgot about it, if you want the truth."

Kate had scribbled all this down as fast as she could. "Thank you, Mr Gregory. Do you have the gallery owner's name?" She could find it herself, but this would save time.

"I knew you'd ask me that, so yes, I do." She could hear the rustle of paper at the end of the line. "He's called Finian Hobbsley. I'll spell it for you." He did so, while Kate wrote it down. "I'm afraid I don't know much about him, to be honest. The work experience was set up by my predecessor, Angela Barry. I can give you her contact details as well, if you like?"

Afterwards, when Kate had thanked him once more and set the headset down, she paused for a moment, replaying the conversation in her head. There had been a moment, just the tiniest moment, when something had felt not quite right. Something so tiny, she couldn't even think of what it had been. Slowly, she drew a question mark on the note pad before her, just after Mark Gregory's name.

She looked up Sea Views on Google. Bit of a cliched name for an art gallery by the sea, Kate thought, and the website itself showed a pleasant but unmemorable gallery. Polished wooden floors, white walls, many framed paintings on the walls. The odd bit of sculpture here and there. The prices, for a small seaside town, seemed quite reasonable, which was the only unusual thing about it. Kate and Anderton had once been to the Affordable Art Fair in London, looking for decoration for their new home. They had come away empty-handed. "I think their definition of affordable differs somewhat from ours," Anderton had remarked drily on the train back to Abbeyford.

The website had little information on it about the owner or manager, whichever Finian Hobbsley was. Kate noted the opening hours and looked at the clock. If she set off now, she could interview him and have a bit of lunch by the seaside, which would be nice.

The morning had been grey and overcast, but the sun was beginning to struggle through the clouds as Kate drove towards the coast. Chloe's house was in Salterton and Kate caught a glimpse of it, a little white cottage looking as if it had been constructed out of sugar cubes. She parked the car in the carpark of the Anchor, a decent pub on the front, deciding on lunch first. It would give her time to do a bit more research and to pull her thoughts together.

She ordered a ploughman's lunch and a lime soda, and settled back in her window seat. Across the road, she could see the sun sparkling off the waves as they rushed and hissed on the stony shore. The tide was going out, gradually, leaving the pebbles it uncovered glossy and new looking as the waves retreated, before they dried and dulled.

Kate took a sip of her drink and opened her notebook. There were more than a few things about this case that were nagging her. Nothing tangible, nothing concrete – more the feelings that, despite them not always coming to anything, she still found hard to dismiss out of hand.

She looked at her notes. Geraint Winner. The younger art student who'd apparently been close friends with Mae – but without any of her closest friends knowing. Or if they had known, why hadn't they mentioned him? Kate wrote *check with Rav* after Geraint's name.

Mark Gregory. Kate looked at the question mark

beside his name, willing whatever had made her note that down to come back to the forefront of her memory. But it didn't. Her pen hovered beside the question mark but, after a moment, she thought better of writing anything. If it was that important, it would come back to her.

Finian Hobbsley. The art gallery owner – manager? – who Mae had, apparently, found 'a bit of a creep'. Kate reminded herself that she only had Mark Gregory's word for that. She made a note to double check with Mae's friends, to see if she'd mentioned anything to them, or to her parents.

Her ploughman's lunch arrived, carried by a smiling young waitress. Kate enjoyed the fresh bread and cheese, and the crisp red apple that accompanied it. There was something to be said for a simple meal, now and again, she thought. She eyed the pickled onion on the plate with regret, knowing that if she gave in and ate it, she'd been risking the most horrendous heartburn. Not to mention that breathing pickled onion fumes over a potential suspect wouldn't be much of a career-enhancing move. Kate checked the clock and realised that she only had an hour left before the gallery shut – although maybe that wouldn't be such a bad thing. Finian Hobbsley might be more talkative without having to deal with customers.

The owner of Sea Views – he was the owner after all – was a tall man of about fifty, with a lot of curly hair, once blonde, now a greyish yellow. He was one of those people in which the bare bones of youthful beauty could still be seen, but submerged now after decades of good – or hard – living. He wore a threadbare tweed jacket and a faded yellow shirt beneath it, buttons straining over a large stomach.

His eyes took on a noticeable twinkle as Kate walked into the gallery, a little bell announcing her arrival. As was usual with a detective, Kate was in plain clothes – maternity plain clothes in her case – and with her bump preceding her (almost as large as Finian Hobbsley's own), she was aware that she didn't look much like a police officer. That could be useful though. In answer to Mr Hobbsley's welcome, spoken in a fruity tone, she produced her warrant card and watched the twinkle in his eye die away immediately.

Chapter Twelve

THERE WERE NO CUSTOMERS IN the gallery, but Hobbsley took Kate into the office at the back of the shop, locking the front door and flipping the hanging sign to 'Closed'. Normally Kate wouldn't have felt much about this but she felt an unexpected frisson of alarm as he did so. Just as quickly, she told herself not to be so stupid. People at the office knew where she was, and she was more than capable of taking care of herself.

It's the twins, she thought silently, as she followed Hobbsley's tweed-clad back through the office door. They make you more vulnerable – in all ways.

The moment of unease dissipated as soon as she was seated. The office itself was small and spectacularly cluttered, but the fitful sun shone in through a large, many-paned window and Finian Hobbsley seated himself across from her and behind a huge, mahogany desk. At least Kate assumed it was a desk, given as its surface was entirely hidden with teetering piles of paper, an empty wine bottle, several overflowing ashtrays, a scarf that Tom Baker would have happily sported when playing Doctor Who, and various other detritus she didn't have enough time to take in properly.

She smiled at Finian Hobbsley and introduced herself. "Thank you for seeing me, Mr Hobbsley. I'm making some enquiries into the disappearance of Mae Denton."

Hobbsley leant back in his chair and folded his hands across his ample stomach. "And whom might that be, Inspector?"

His tone was polite but puzzled. Kate repeated the name. "Mae Denton? She's the young woman who's been missing from her home in Abbeyford for the last two weeks."

His expression of confusion remained. "Mae Denton? No, the name—" Something seemed to occur to him. "Oh, my goodness, the young lady on the news? Is that the one?" Repressing a sharp retort, Kate confirmed that it was. "Well, how very *silly* of me, I didn't make the connection. Yes, I have heard of her, one of my clients was talking about her just the other day."

"Your clients?"

Hobbsley smiled. "Yes, I take on private commissions, portraits, and so forth. I'm an artist myself, of course. That's where the real money is, you know. I'm afraid my little gallery is something of a *hobby*, in terms of the cash it makes."

He laughed and Kate forced herself to smile. "So, you are aware of Mae's disappearance, sir?"

Hobbsley immediately became serious. "Well, yes, but only by what I've *heard*, of course. How can I help?"

"I understand that she did some work experience here for you, last year?"

With an astonished expression, Hobbsley sat forward. "*Here*? That poor young lady? Are you sure?"

Kate nodded. "I have confirmation from the Abbeyford College of Art and Design that she – Mae – and one of her fellow students, Johnny Papmier, undertook two weeks of work experience here in the gallery. In June, last year?" She held out the printed emails from the college confirming the placement.

Finian Hobbsley took them, shaking his head slowly. "Well, I'm not sure—" He ran his eye over the pieces of paper. "Well, - ah, yes, Johnny *Papmier* – yes, I do remember – unusual name, isn't it? But Mae? Well, there was a very pretty girl here at that time – I think – but I can't remember her name." He handed back the emails to Kate with an attempt at a hearty smile, which didn't quite reach his eyes. "I suppose it must have been her, if you say it was. My memory's not what it was, I'm afraid."

Kate folded the papers back into her handbag. "We're trying to find out anything about Mae's background, anything really, that might help us find her.

As I'm sure you can appreciate, her family are extremely distressed by her disappearance."

Hobbsley looked troubled. "Well, yes, of *course* they would be. I can quite understand that." He rubbed a hand along his stubbly jaw. "But my dear young lady, I'm really not sure how I can help. It seems, from your, your *papers*, that Mae did work here for a little bit, but I'm blessed if I can really remember much about her. As far as I can recall, she was a pleasant enough girl."

Kate watched him. "Did you and she ever work late together? Would she have confided in you if there was something bothering her?"

Hobbsley looked, if possible, even more astonished. "Work together? Confide in me? My dear Inspector, I barely *knew* the girl."

"Is there anyone else who works here that might be able to help us with our enquiries?"

"Oh no, I'm afraid it's just me. There's not a lot of footfall, around here, you know. As I said, the bulk of my income comes from private commissions and sales."

"Are you able to give me any names of your customers? Anyone who might have spoken to Mae whilst she was here?" Kate was clutching at straws here a little, but any shot was worth a try, in her opinion.

Hobbsley went from astonishment to anger. "My *clients*? Inspector, how on earth would they be able to help?"

"It's a standard enquiry, Mr Hobbsley. I'm not casting any aspersions on your clients; I'd simply like to know if Mae ever spoke to them."

"Well, I can't imagine why. She and Johnny were in the backroom, mostly – not this office, the storeroom where I keep most of the stock." His voice reverted back to the unctuous tone he'd previously employed. "I tend to be *front of house*, as it were. My customers appreciate the personal touch, and I didn't think a couple of sixth formers would be very helpful in a service role."

Kate thought he was something of a pretentious fool but kept her thoughts to herself. She forced herself to smile. "So, you don't believe you have the name of anyone who might have spoken to Mae while she worked here?"

"I'm afraid not, Inspector." Hobbsley managed a twinkle at her once more. "As far as I can recall, the two of them mostly sorted out paintings, dealt with a few orders, that sort of thing."

"Could I see the storeroom please?"

Hobbsley's thick eyebrows went up. "If you think it's necessary."

There wasn't much to see – a rather bare room with a concrete floor, paintings stacked around the walls. Some were covered in dustsheets, whilst others were plain to see. Kate pointed at one of the ones covered up, a large four-foot by four-foot canvas.

"What's that one?"

"One of my recent commissions. I'm not yet finished with it." Hobbsley twinkled at her once more. "I'm afraid I can't let you see it yet, Inspector. Not least because it's currently in something of a *mess*. I'll have to do some work on it later."

Kate nodded. "I'm guessing you can't tell me who it's for either?"

Hobbsley winked at her. "Well, that would be telling. But I can tell you that several of the local council members *have* commissioned a few paintings for the council offices. They believe in supporting local businesses."

"I see. Do you ever sell artwork from the college? From its students?"

Hobbsley looked taken aback. "From students? My goodness me, no. Forgive me, dear Inspector, but honestly, the talent churned out by most of our local art colleges... well, I say *talent*. Let's just say, I'm not expecting to discover the next Hockney. Not even the next Damien Hurst," he added, with an eloquent sniff.

Kate had almost had enough of his posturing. She probed a little deeper about his attitude to Mae, whether he'd ever spent some time with her alone, to be met with the expected denials.

As was standard procedure, Kate asked for his whereabouts over the days since Mae had been missing. There was nothing very illuminating – Finian Hobbsley appeared to lead a quiet life. The only social engagement he'd had since Mae had disappeared had been a drinks party at one of the said local councillor's house, a Margery Bamberth. Kate took down what details she could and decided that was as much as she was going to be able to get from this witness at this stage.

She thanked the gallery owner and took her leave, waddling back to her car. Having been on her feet for a while, her back was aching badly, the tendons in her pelvis stretched and sore. She found a café halfway back to where her car was parked and went inside, gratefully subsiding onto a chair and ordered a fat slice of chocolate cake to go with her camomile tea. She ate slowly, watching the hypnotic movement of the waves on the beach, the rush and drag of the water sparkling under the weak, late-winter sun.

Chapter Thirteen

The first thing Kate did the next morning was corner Rav at his desk. She noted he didn't look quite as exhausted as he had done for the past few weeks, and said as much.

"Jarina's taken the kids to her mum's for a few days," was the explanation. "I'm basically going home from work and getting straight into bed every night. Catching up on sleep."

Kate looked at him. "Everything all right between you two?"

Rav looked surprised. "Yeah. Yeah, of course." Then he looked worried. "Why'd you ask?"

Kate felt foolish. "Oh, nothing. Ignore me." She fell back on the excuse she was in danger of using a little bit too often. "Pregnancy brain."

Rav grinned at her. "Just you wait."

"Oh, don't."

"Sorry. Now I'm getting some sleep, I'm getting my banter back."

Kate huffed in mock-indignation. "Now you sound like Theo."

"Who does?" asked Theo from across the room.

"Doesn't matter." Kate hauled her attention back to the matter in hand. "Anyway, I wanted to ask you about Geraint Winner. Presumably you interviewed him yesterday?"

Rav immediately became serious. "Yeah, I did. Sit down and we'll go through it."

Internally, Kate raised her eyebrows. This sounded promising... She did as she was told and subsided onto a spare chair, trying not to grunt as she took the weight off her feet.

"Yeah, so," said Rav, reaching for his notebook. "Geraint Winner. He's a little pipsqueak of a guy – what?" he asked, as Kate giggled.

"Just the word. It's so – retro."

"But you know what I mean, right? Yeah?" At Kate's nod, Rav went on. "Right, he's small, seems younger than his age, I'm guessing he's gay. Think he's doing something with – what is it? Textiles? Anyway, the fashion side of it."

"Right," said Kate, nodding.

"Well, I asked him about Mae, obviously, and he was – well, pretty cagey. More cagey than I think he should have been. Very nervous, you know?"

"Right," said Kate, again. Then feeling she should be contributing more, she added, "Why do you think that was?"

Rav shrugged. "It could just be he's not had much

to do with the police. Could be. Then again, I got the impression he was keeping something back."

"Hmm." Kate pondered. "Did he seem like he'd had a relationship with Mae? I mean, a sexual one?"

Rav screwed up his face in thought. "Well, no, not really. But they clearly knew each other and hung out together. As I said, I think he's gay."

"That means nothing," called Theo, from across the room. Both Rav and Kate looked at him.

"What do you mean?" asked Kate.

"Gay, straight – doesn't mean anything anymore. They'll do anyone. *They* – you know. They don't even say he or she anymore."

Both Rav and Kate regarded Theo for a long moment. Then, ignoring him, they turned back to face each other again. "So, why did Geraint say that none of Mae's friends appeared to know about him?" asked Kate, which was the question that was really bugging her.

Rav shrugged. "I did ask him. He said they weren't really interested in hanging out with him, being older and all that."

Kate frowned. "But he can't be more than a year younger, surely?"

"That's what I thought. But that's what he said. Also, he said that Johnny Papmier didn't like him much, so he just used to see Mae on her own."

"Why didn't he like Geraint?"

"I don't know. From what he said, he implied it was homophobia."

"Bollocks," Theo called from across the room.

"Would you shut up?" snapped Kate, and he subsided, giggling.

Rav raised a hand, palm up. "Theo may have a point. Gen Z are not normally known for their bigotry, are they?"

"That doesn't mean it doesn't exist." Kate sat back in her chair, stretching out her spine. "But I get what you're saying. Okay, file him away for now, under 'may need to be interviewed again at a later date'. And go back to Mae's friends, see what they say about him."

"Will do."

Kate patted him on the shoulder and heaved herself out of her chair. She had one of her pre-natal appointments that afternoon, just a standard checkup, but she could feel apprehension beginning to tighten her stomach. She could never see the flickering, grainy images of the babies on the sonographer's screen without her own heart thumping. What if they found something wrong? What if one of the babies or both had d– but no, she couldn't ever finish *that* thought in words, even internal words. Just the beginning of the thought seemed to break her into pieces.

Months more of this to endure...and then, recalling something her mother, of all people, had said to her once, the worry never leaves you... Why in hell had she signed up to this, honestly? Biology had a lot to answer for.

"You okay?"

Kate came back to earth, or specifically, the office. Chloe was just sitting down across from her with a quizzical look on her face.

"I'm fine." Kate shoved gloomy speculation away from her and sat up a little. "Are you okay?"

Chloe half smiled. "Me? Yes. Why wouldn't I be?"

"Oh, ignore me." Kate filled her friend in on the conversation she'd just had with Rav. Chloe looked as unimpressed as Theo had been.

"There's something funny going on at that college if you ask me."

Kate, who'd dropped her gaze to her desk and the multitude of reports she had to read, brought her head up with a jolt. "Ow. What do you mean?"

"Oh, don't get excited. I haven't any *evidence*. Just what you'd call a feeling." Chloe's eyes met Kate's. "They're all hiding something, that lot. All of them."

There was a moment of silence. "You think whatever it is has something to do with Mae's disappearance?" Kate said, slowly.

Chloe gave a very Theo-like shrug. "Could be. Might not be. Who knows?"

"Hmm." Kate sat back in her chair for a moment, thinking. She looked up and saw that, for once, Olbeck was in his office and not on the phone. "Come with me for a moment. Let's run things through with Mark."

Chloe got up obediently. Kate went to knock on the glass wall of Olbeck's office.

"Anything new?" he asked as he admitted them.

Kate waved at Chloe to speak, which she did, reiterating what she'd just told Kate.

Olbeck frowned. "When you say all of them, do you mean the staff as well?"

Chloe half laughed. "I don't exactly know what I mean. It's just, I get the distinct impression that everyone is hiding something. Or keeping something back, at least."

"Come on Chloe, how long have you been an officer for? You know as well as I do that, they always hold something back. Our job is to see if it's relevant or not." Pretending exasperation, Olbeck looked across at Kate. "What do you think?"

Out of nowhere, Kate recalled the tiny wrong note she'd encountered in her interview with Mark Gregory, Mae's teacher. "I know what Chloe means. I've just remembered something. It sounds ridiculously minor, I know, but when I was interviewing Mae's tutor, he stumbled over a word, hesitated is more like it, just a very minor word." She silently thanked the heavens that she'd brought her notebook along already and wouldn't have to waddle back to get it. "It's here." She paused and reread what she'd written down at the interview. Now she was confronted with it, it didn't seem so very important – or indeed, worthy of comment.

"Go on," said Olbeck.

"Well – it's nothing really—" Kate caught the look from both Chloe and Olbeck and hurried on. "It was just, Mark Gregory, Mae's tutor; right at the end he said something a bit odd. Just very slightly." She looked again over her notes. "He said Mae was free to be friends with whomever she wanted to be. And then he kind of paused..." She trailed off.

"Is that it?" asked Olbeck.

"I did say it wasn't much—"

"No, I get it," said Chloe. "It *is* a bit of an odd thing to say, about a student. I don't know, almost – a rebuttal?"

"What?"

"I mean, it could be interpreted as him, Gregory, having been accused of – I don't know... interfering in Mae's friendships?"

"No, it doesn't," said Olbeck, by now properly exasperated.

"I wasn't suggesting anything," offered Kate. "I can't describe it, it just struck a wrong note for me, that's all. Very, very slightly."

"Hmm." Olbeck didn't sound convinced. Kate was reminded of when Anderton used to sit across from her, giving the same sort of dubious response to her sometimes rather wildcat suggestions. She was pierced with a mixture of nostalgia, amusement and longing.

"Anyway," Chloe was saying, and Kate dragged herself back to the present. The memory of Anderton reminded her of her scan and she cast an anxious glance at the clock, realising she would have to leave soon to meet him at the hospital.

"Well, just dig into what you can find—"

"We still don't have the connection between Geraint Winner and Mae – if it was anything else other than friendship—"

Olbeck and Chloe were talking over each other, but Kate hardly heard them. She stood up and excused herself, reminding them that she had an appointment. She caught the anxious glance that Olbeck sent her but refused to acknowledge it. She had no capacity for dealing with anyone else's apprehension apart from her own.

Chapter Fourteen

"Home?" Anderton took Kate's arm as the electronic doors of the hospital reception released them into the chilly afternoon air. Light was draining out of the day. Darkness coalesced in the cloudy sky, but Kate was feeling warm, lit up with relief and happiness. Everything with the scan had been fine; the two babies obligingly performing for the camera with wriggles and kicks. In her handbag was the scan picture, in a twee little folder printed with the inaccurate legend *My First Picture* (this was the twins' third picture at least).

She hugged Anderton's arm to her. "Let's go out to eat, celebrate a bit."

He looked pleased. "Why not?"

"I might allow myself a thimbleful of champagne," Kate said, just to see his expression, and laughed. "Of course not. Leaving aside anything else, it'll give me raging heartburn."

They drove to one of the more expensive restaurants in the vicinity of Abbeyford, Bailey's. It was nearby and, as Kate had suggested, they both felt like celebrating the continued good health of their babies. As they walked into the grand foyer (Bailey's was a hotel as well as a restaurant), Kate made a mental note to herself that they really *did* need to start reigning it in a little, money-wise. She would soon be on maternity leave – *please, God*, she added to herself, automatically – which meant a big drop in income and there would be two babies to take care of as well, double the cost of everything. She had so far refused to think about how much two full-time nursery places would be.

Pushing that thought away once more, Kate settled in to enjoy her dinner. In such a high-end restaurant, there was of course no television to be seen in the room, but as they sat down, she caught sight of a newspaper folded on the adjourning table. *No New Leads in Mae D* was all she could see, as a crumpled napkin obscured the rest of the headline, but it was obvious what was hidden. Kate frowned and shifted her chair a little so she could no longer see it.

She tried to switch her attention back to the lovely surroundings and her equally lovely partner.

"I came here with Andrew once," she said, as they unfolded their own white linen napkins.

"Who? Oh, Andrew Stanton? Did you?" Anderton thought for a moment. "Christ, when was that?"

"Literally *years* ago." Kate was silent for a moment, thinking. "Oh God, it was during the Butterfly case. Remember that?"

Anderton gave her an old-fashioned look. "I'm hardly likely to have forgotten *that*, am I? And surely, you of all people haven't?"

She hadn't done it for years, but now Kate's hand automatically went to the ridged scar on her back, the long-healed remnant of her fight with a killer. She saw Anderton noticed her doing so and laughed, awkwardly, removing her hand. "I hadn't forgotten. It's a long time ago, now."

"Your first serial killer case, wasn't it?"

Kate made a noise of agreement. "Mmm. And hopefully my last."

"Well, God knows we all hope that, but it's unlikely."

Kate made her agreeing noise again.

The two of them were silent for a moment, their eyes downcast. Then Anderton added, "Some things probably are best forgotten."

The waiter came up to the table then with a bottle of champagne. Kate, who'd been in the loo when Anderton had ordered it, raised her eyebrows but welcomed the diversion.

"I was joking about that."

"I know", said Anderton, grinning. "It's all for me. You can drive home."

"Oi…" Kate felt her heart lift a little at the return to cheerful normality.

"Will Madam be wanting a glass?" asked the waiter, with a pointed look at Kate's bump.

The devil inside Kate whispered *go on, have one just to piss him off*. Back in the real world, Kate smiled and shook her head. "No, thank you."

Once the waiter had glided off to shame some other customer, Anderton leant over and poured a tiny amount into Kate's empty water glass. "Go on. A mouthful won't do any harm."

They clinked glasses and drank. "To our little ones," said Anderton, and Kate was touched. He wasn't normally sentimental.

As they waited for their food, Kate took out the scan photo again and they both took it in turns to peruse it.

"You know," said Anderton when it was his turn to look. "I'm sure one of them is a boy. Look, you can definitely see a penis."

The words were barely out of his mouth when the supercilious waiter returned with their food. This time it was Anderton's turn to get the pointed look. Kate chewed the inside of her cheek to stop herself from laughing.

"Let me see," she said, as the waiter walked away again, allowing herself to giggle.

They argued amiably over the possibility of the baby's sex as they ate. "You *can* see it," insisted Anderton, gesturing with his fork. "Clearly takes after his old man."

"For God's sake, would you stop talking about genitalia," said Kate, deliberately timing it for when the waiter returned to check if everything was all right with their meal. "Fine, thanks," Anderton responded in a strangled voice and when the waiter left once more, the two of them collapsed.

"The poor guy," gasped Kate, when she could speak. "They'll be chucking us out in a minute—"

"Save me from paying the bill," said Anderton and they collapsed once more, trying to stifle their laughter.

By the time the dessert menu was frostily proffered, both Kate and Anderton had composed themselves. Kate couldn't manage more than a couple of mouthfuls of her chocolate mousse.

"That's a shame," said Anderton, clearly meaning it. He then spoilt it by adding, "I'll finish it. Heave it over."

Kate handed it to him with some regret. At least it wasn't Theo sitting opposite, who would have made it his life's mission to eat it in the most over-the-top, annoying way ever. She took a sip of her not-very-satisfying decaffeinated coffee instead.

The couple who had been dining next to them got up and left, leaving behind the newspaper with the headline about Mae Denton. This time, it caught Anderton's eye.

"Still no more news?" he asked.

Kate mock-frowned at him. "You know I can't discuss it with you."

"I know, I know. But we don't have to discuss it. Not as in *speculate*."

"Well, then..."

Anderton scraped the last of the mousse from the crystal dish. "I mean, what we could do is sit here and I could talk. You wouldn't have to say anything, join in at all. Just listen."

This time Kate frowned for real, although more in curiosity than anger. "We can't say anything that might prejudice the case."

"Oh darling, honestly. I do know that, I was a bloody DCI for decades." He shook his head at her. "I'm hardly going to put our conversation on Twitter, am I? I just meant, I'll talk, and you listen. That's all."

The waiter came back with the bill, but this time they ignored him apart from a muttered 'thanks' from Anderton.

"Go on," said Kate, once the waiter had left.

"Well, I've been thinking about it, to be honest."

"Who hasn't?"

"Well, yes. The wall-to-wall coverage hasn't helped." A thought seemed to strike him. "You haven't heard from young Tin, have you?"

"Tin?" Kate was so busy thinking of Mae Denton that for a moment she had to struggle to think who he meant. "Tin? Oh, no. Why would I?"

"I just thought – with that article—"

"I don't think he'd come to me," said Kate, immediately doubting herself. Tin *had* accosted her in the course of her job before, and a fine row they'd had over it at the time. "Mark's doing regular press conferences," she added, out loud.

"Poor bugger," said Anderton. "God, how I used to hate those. Anyway, I wonder whether he will. Tin, I mean – contact you."

"I'll cross that bridge if and when I come to it." Kate gave up on her coffee and pushed it aside. "Let's not borrow trouble."

"Well, quite. Anyway. Mae Denton. I was thinking about the proximity of the quarry to the river. I know there's been a cursory search..."

"That's not true," said Kate, forgetting she was supposed to be keeping quiet. "We've had frog men down there and a sonar search. They didn't find anything."

"Oh. Right, must have missed that in the reporting. It was just an idea, anyway."

"Thank you." Kate tried to sound grateful. She suddenly felt swamped with fatigue.

Anderton noticed. "Ah, you've hit a wall, haven't you love? Come on, let's get you and the babies home."

"Okay," Kate yawned.

Anderton patted her stomach as she put on her coat. "Home, son. Home, gender-neutral."

Kate gave him a look, but she couldn't help smiling. They made their way back out to the car and drove home under a clear sky and a canopy of stars.

Chapter Fifteen

Anderton's powers of prescience were given a rather startling endorsement the next morning, when the very first phone call that Kate received was from Tin Johnson himself.

Kate had paid, rather unfairly she thought, for the last night's sumptuous meal. Although she'd quickly fallen asleep when she and Anderton had got home, heartburn and nausea had woken her up at about three o'clock in the morning. She'd spent most of the rest of the night in the bathroom in some misery, interspersed with snatched half hours of trying to get some more sleep. She was therefore not well prepared to deal with Tin's voice on the telephone, when she finally dragged herself to the office.

"Hi, Kate. It's Tin here, Tin Johnson. Remember me?"

Kate had answered the phone whilst confronting her ghostly (in more ways than one) reflection in her computer monitor – she hadn't got up the energy to turn it on yet. She snapped out of her stupor with a jolt that made Chloe look up from her desk in surprise. "Tin?"

He had the same nice voice and easy manner, something that had suited him well in his journalistic career. "It's me. Long time, hey? How are you?"

"I'm fine, fine thanks. Fine. How are you?"

"Yeah, I'm all good. Back in the UK now for a bit."

"Good, good, I'm fine, thanks," stuttered Kate, and then got a grip on herself. "Ahem, sorry. Bit of a hectic morning—"

"I can call back—"

"No, it's fine." Chloe was unashamedly listening by now. Kate poked her tongue out at her and turned her attention back to the call. "How are you?" Too late, she remembered, she'd already asked that.

Tim chuckled. "I'm good. Anyway, I was hoping you might be free for a drink sometime?"

Immediately, Kate's hackles went up. "If you've got a question on the case – whatever case that might be, you can ask me here and now, Tin."

"Hey, don't be like that. I meant it would be nice to catch up. That's all."

Given that Tin was an investigative journalist, Kate took that with a barrowload of salt. But she was intrigued enough not to dismiss his request out of hand. For one thing, there was curiosity to see what time had made of him. And, with past cases when she'd been with him as his girlfriend, she remembered he could sometimes come up with something useful, some contact or some piece of information hitherto unknown to the police.

"Oh, right. Well, yes, that would be nice." Kate thought she should be saying more than that, but she was momentarily stuck for words.

"Is the Black Cat still going?" That was where they'd had their first date – or meeting, anyway.

"Er, yes. Yes, it is."

"Excellent. Are you free later?"

Annoyingly, Kate was. Where was pregnancy yoga when you needed it? "Er—"

"No worries, if not. I'm around for a bit."

What did that mean? Was he just back in the UK for a trip or had he moved back? "No, it's fine—" Once again, Kate got a grip on herself. "Tonight's fine. Just let me—" She caught herself and repeated her words. "Tonight's fine. About eight?"

"Cool. See you then, Kate. Looking forward to it!"

After he'd rung off, Kate put the receiver down and turned to face Chloe's raised eyebrows. She couldn't help laughing.

"Date with an old flame?"

"How did you guess?"

Chloe looked even more intrigued. "I was actually joking, you daft bint. Is it, seriously?"

Kate explained. Chloe knew Tin and – now Kate remembered – had actually warned Kate off going to New York to live with him. Good advice, given how things had worked out...

"How's Anderton going to take that?" was Chloe's next question.

Kate laughed, although she was slightly annoyed. "It's one bloody drink, Chloe, to see if he actually has anything useful to tell us. Anderton will completely understand that." She added, "Besides, in case you haven't noticed, I'm massively pregnant."

"So, if you weren't, you'd be having an affair?" asked Chloe, but she was grinning as she said it. Kate flicked her the bird, grinning back and got up to take her mobile into the corridor. Sanguine as she was about Anderton's reaction to the news that she was going for a drink with her old boyfriend, she felt she owed it to him to have that conversation in relative privacy.

The afternoon dragged and for that, Kate was glad. Although she wasn't that worried about seeing Tin (and part of her was gleefully anticipating his reaction once he saw her pregnancy), it was still a meeting which she wasn't able to approach with complete equanimity. Anderton had been agreeable about it, but he'd signed off from their call with "Enjoy yourself but be careful." Kate had at first taken that as a warning not to reveal anything that might later turn up in the press. But had he actually meant for her to watch her behaviour around Tin, in case he thought – well, that there were still feelings there? On either or both sides? Surely not? But just the idea of it made Kate feel a little anxious and cross. It didn't help that the twins could clearly feel the tension and kept rolling about and kicking her, until she was tempted to poke them and shout 'stop it, you two!'. She resisted. Raising your voice to a couple of unborn babies was frowned upon and, God help her, she probably needed to reserve all the shouting at her kids for the future.

Gradually, the office emptied out around her. Kate worked through some casefiles she'd been neglecting in favour of the Mae Denton case. With regards to that, she felt like leaving it alone for one night. She had nothing else to contribute to whatever it was that they already knew. Perhaps Tin would have something that might come in handy? It was a faint hope, but wasn't everything about this case a faint hope at the moment?

At about seven fifteen, Kate heaved herself up and went to the Ladies, to neaten her hair and swipe on some lipstick. She didn't look particularly blooming today, she had to admit. The shattered sleep of the night before and the wearying day had made her look pale and washed out. Kate tried to pinch some colour back to her cheeks before giving it up as a bad job. Tin would have to take her as he found her, not that she cared much anyway. As the last one to leave the office, she locked the door behind her and made her way to the lift.

The Black Cat was only a ten-minute stroll from the police station, but she'd left herself double the time needed so she could walk slowly. As she made her way there, Kate felt her thoughts slip back to Mae. She had been missing for over three weeks now and they were still nowhere near to a conclusion. Not even a solid theory as to why she was missing. No body. No real motive for her disappearance as yet. No one *really* behaving suspiciously, despite Chloe's misgivings about the college. All Kate had were whispers of intuition, niggles and half-remembered words...

Darkness had fallen completely by now and the streetlights shone orange against the black sky. Looking up at them, Kate could see a faint drizzle beginning to fall, feeling it on her face and hair. She wrapped her coat more firmly over her bump and quickened her pace.

Chapter Sixteen

KATE HAD, AT TIMES IN her relationship with Tin, found him somewhat annoying. This feeling returned to her that evening when she entered the Black Cat and saw him at the bar, having the gall to not look a day older than when she'd last seen him all those years ago. He was dressed in what she privately termed to herself 'New York finery' and the only change that immediately struck her was the gold wedding ring on his left hand.

At that moment, he turned and saw her, and she was rewarded by him doing a literal double take.

"Shit, Kate," he said, as she came up to him. "Erm – congratulations!"

"Thanks," Kate said, demurely.

"I was going to say you're looking well but, bloody hell, you're looking better than well." Tin gave her an awkward hug to avoid the bump. "When are you due?"

Kate told him. She could tell he was trying to find a delicate way of asking 'whose is it?' and decided that he could wait just a *little* longer to be enlightened.

"Erm – can I get you a drink? Soft drink?"

"I'll have a gin and tonic, actually," said Kate, just to see the look on his face. Then she said, laughing, "I'm joking, idiot. I'll have a lemonade."

"I'll get it. Er - you - well, you sit down."

"Thanks." Kate patted her bump. "Carrying quite a load here!" She waddled to a free table, smirking to herself.

The bar was fairly empty, it being a weeknight and Tin was soon back with the drinks. He'd got himself what looked like a whisky and soda.

"Cheers, then."

"Cheers."

"How—"

"What have you—"

They spoke over each other and laughed, and that broke the tension somewhat.

"I'll start," said Tin. "Well - I'm - it's so good to see you but God, that gave me a surprise. So, you're married now?"

"Not yet. Engaged though." Kate didn't wear an engagement ring. Chloe had told her she was mad not to have one, that it was the perfect time to get a nice bit of jewellery, but Kate didn't feel comfortable with the connotations. *I have to get you something*, Anderton had said. *Why*, Kate had asked, and he'd been unable to answer. In the end, they'd bought each other a present – a new set of golf clubs for Anderton from Kate, and a giant Monstera Deliciosa for Kate from Anderton, which towered in the corner of the living room like a more benign version of the plant from The Little Shop of Horrors.

All this passed through Kate's mind in an instant as Tin said, "Oh, right. Great. Well, congratulations again."

A silence fell between them. Tin looked at Kate meaningfully. She knew damn well she was expected to tell him who she was engaged to, but it was just too much fun dragging it out...

"I know you're married," she said, smiling. "Do you guys live in the States still?"

"Yeah, New York still. Angie's a lawyer."

"Oh, right."

Another silence. Kate took pity on him. "Anderton and I moved house not that long ago—"

"Anderton? You're with him now?"

"For years now," Kate said, laughing to disguise a spurt of annoyance. "We're planning to get married once the babies are born."

"*Babies*? You mean there's more than one in there? My God—"

The resulting discussion took them all the way through the second round of drinks, and the arrival of a bowl of giant green olives glistening with olive oil. Kate heard that Tin and his wife had no children of their own, but Tin's daughter Celeste was now halfway through a master's degree in Edinburgh. Kate listened, making all the right noises, and felt old. Celeste had been, what, six or so when Kate and Tin had been a couple?

Finally, Tin sat back and fixed Kate with a look that, despite the years, she recognised immediately.

"So?" she asked, unable to help herself.

"So?" Tin laughed. "I was just about to say that."

"I know. What is it that you really want, Tin?"

Tin looked hurt. "Why would you say that? It's been nice to catch up, hasn't it?"

"Come on, don't treat me like an idiot. I saw that article you wrote. You're looking for an angle on Mae Denton, aren't you?"

Tin's dark eyes gleamed. "Do you have one?"

Kate's laugh this time was a little more forced. "There've been plenty of press conferences, Tin. I assume you've attended some of them?"

"Come on, Kate, I know there's always more to what the cops are telling us."

"Well, what makes you think I'd share that with you?" Kate said, sharply. "If, *if*, there was anything. Which there's not."

Tin gave her a look which meant he was not convinced. For a moment, he said nothing but picked up his empty glass and inclined it towards her. "Want another?"

"Yes. Thank you." Kate accepted to give herself a little time to think. As Tin was at the bar, she seriously contemplated walking out. How stupid to think that he wouldn't want privileged information from her, despite her telling him numerous times when they were together that she couldn't discuss anything with him. Jesus, she didn't even talk things through with Anderton anymore and he had *been* a police officer. By the time Tin came back with drinks for them both, she was thoroughly annoyed.

"Listen—" she began, trying to keep the edge from her tone, when Tin interrupted her.

"I suppose you think I only asked you to here to get a scoop on the case?"

"What—" was all Kate managed before Tin spoke again.

"I'm not *that* bad, Kate. I know I treated you pretty shittily at times but that's in the past." He held her gaze. "I didn't ask you here to see if you could give me anything."

There was a short silence while Kate fought for control of her voice. "You didn't?" was what she managed after a moment.

"No, I didn't." Tin took a sip of his drink. He was on his third whiskey and the alcohol was beginning to put a glaze on his eyes, although he sounded perfectly clear and competent.

"Oh." Kate groped for something else to say before realising she had nothing.

"I actually wanted to tell *you* something."

Kate paused with her glass of lemonade halfway to her mouth. "Oh?" Tin nodded. Kate raised her eyebrows. "Yes?"

Tin looked away. "I've got a daughter myself, you know." Kate *did* know, having just spent at least half an hour talking about Celeste with her father. Perhaps he was drunker than he appeared.

"Yes?" She said again, nodding encouragingly.

Tin cleared his throat. "Have you made any official connection between Mae's disappearance and the disappearance of Saskia Devonshire?"

Kate, who'd been taking a sip from her glass, felt herself still. She put the glass down slowly. "With Saskia Devonshire?"

Tin could tell she was playing for time. "I know you know who I'm talking about."

"Why do you ask?"

"Because I believe I might have some information on her that the police might not be privy too."

Kate tensed further. "What information?"

Tin looked away. "Did you know that Saskia was a life model?"

"A what?" The words were out of Kate's mouth before she had thought about it. Of course she knew what a life model was, what was the matter with her? "I mean, I'm sorry – Saskia was a life model?"

Tin nodded. "Her parents kept it quiet. You know, they're a pretty traditional family and it wasn't the sort of thing they were proud of their daughter doing..." He caught her gaze again. "Did you know?"

Kate wavered, torn between honesty and ego.

"Well – I don't have the file right in front of me at the moment, Tin, in case you hadn't noticed..."

He smirked. "I'm guessing that's a 'no', then."

"All right," Kate snapped. "No, I'm not aware that was known. Does it matter?"

"You tell me. Wasn't Mae Denton an art student?" He caught Kate's expression and added hastily, "I mean, is. Is an art student?"

"Yes, but—" At that moment, one of the twins rushing off the sugary lemonade gave her a great kick in the belly. "*Oof.* Ow."

Tin looked concerned. "Are you okay?"

Kate rubbed her stomach. "I'm fine, fine. Go on." Tin hesitated once more, and she gestured impatiently with her free hand. "Seriously, go on."

"Okay. Well, I've been following up on the investigations into all four girls' disappearance." He caught Kate's frown and added, hastily, "Well, as you know. You saw the original article."

"Yes, I did."

"The article—" Tin hesitated for a moment. "I didn't mean it to come out as quite so critical of the police as it did. The editor did a bit of a hatchet job before it went out."

Kate didn't believe him, but she wasn't going to get caught up in an argument. "Go on with what you were saying about Saskia Devonshire."

"Right." Tin finished his third whiskey, but Kate didn't offer to go and get more. She wanted him coherent. "Well, like I said, Saskia did some life modelling—"

"At Abbeyford College?" Kate couldn't believe that they would have missed that if that were the case.

"No, somewhere in Wallingham, I think. Anyway, she only did a few classes and it's probably nothing, but what with Mae being an art student, and everything – well, I thought you ought to know. Might be worth looking into?"

"Hmm." Kate realised she sounded ungrateful and hastened to add, "But thank you. I'll certainly bring it to the DCI's attention." Tin was looking at her as if he expected something more and she added, trying not to sound grudging, "Honestly, thanks. It's probably nothing but we'll certainly follow it up."

There didn't seem to be much to say after that. Kate thanked him for the drinks, reiterated (rather mendaciously) that it had been good to catch up, and took her leave, promising (again mendaciously) to keep in touch. She drove home, thinking about Saskia Devonshire and Mae Denton. Could this be a link between them that she'd been looking for? Or was it just a coincidence? And even if it was a link, did it actually mean anything? She was tired now, the twins kicking her unmercifully and she parked the car and plodded towards the front door, dismissing the evening from her mind.

Chapter Seventeen

IT WAS DARK IN THE room, but not the darkness of the blindfold. This darkness was the benign type, the normal darkness of an evening. There was no window in the room, but somehow darkness crept in, under the heavy door or through the cracks in the walls.

Mae lay on the only piece of furniture in the room, the chaise-longue covered in gold silk. Chaise-longue... she was proud of herself for remembering the correct name. When she had first regained consciousness, when reality had come flooding in, the panic and terror she'd felt had been so bad she'd almost forgotten her own name. Now, after all the time here, she was calmer. A little calmer. Able to remember words.

Chaise-longue... she hadn't actually remembered the name, now she thought about it. *He* had said it, one of the times he'd been in the room. *Get on the chaise longue. Stretch out your arms. Lift one leg.* Mae, remembering, turned her face into the cold silk, huddling herself into a ball. It was cold in the room, a dampish feeling to the walls, and she was dressed in a silk gown. Silk on silk. It made it hard to stay in one place on the chaise-longue.

The handcuff on her wrist weighed her arm down. The inside of the cuff was padded, lined with velvet that was that beautiful colour between green and blue, unseen now in the darkness. Lined so as not to mark her wrist, Mae assumed. She'd torn at it with her other hand, once she'd woken up that first time, but had succeeded in nothing else but tearing her fingernails. That had made him angry, and she hadn't eaten that day. The food she was given was light and delicate, hardly enough to sustain a person, but it was food and, deprived of it, she had wept with hunger for the next two days.

Sleep. Go back to sleep. Sleep was safe, sleep was comfort. Sleep was dreams of her family and her home and of freedom. But it was hard to sleep now, having slept so much before. Mae felt hot tears flood her eyes and pushed her face further into the slippery back of the sofa, wanting to block out the darkness, both surrounding her and in her own head.

PART TWO

Chapter Eighteen

EARLY TO HER DESK THAT morning, Kate had the office to herself for half an hour, which was pleasing. She fetched the file on Saskia Devonshire and sat down with it and a cup of herbal tea. Boy, she was sick of herbal tea. The first thing she was going to do after birth was down a pint of coffee. Full-strength, caffeinated, kick-like-a-mule coffee. You probably won't, she told herself and couldn't help but smile. "It's a goal," she said out loud, chuckling.

She had, of course, read the file on Saskia's disappearance several times but this time she went through it slowly and carefully. As she suspected, there was no mention of the girl working as a life model. Had Tin been telling her the truth? But why would he lie? Kate might not fully trust him, but she did know that he respected her enough to not send her on a wild goose chase. As people began to trickle into the office, Kate closed the folder and stared ahead, wondering what to do next.

Olbeck wasn't in the office that morning and Kate was unsure whether he was off for the day or just been caught up in meetings or something like that. She texted him a request for a quick catch up when he had the time and then put her phone away, wondering what to do next.

"Morning, bird," said Chloe, sitting down opposite her.

"Morning," replied Kate, absently. After a moment, she cleared a space on her desk and pulled a blank piece of paper towards her. Mind map it, that was the thing. Kate liked to see things written out in black and white.

On one side of the paper, she wrote *Mae Denton*. On the other, she wrote *Saskia Devonshire*. Beneath each she wrote *disappeared, nineteen years old, white, middle-class, female.* The only things they both ostensibly had in common.

But was that true? Saskia had apparently worked as a life model – an artistic job. Mae Denton *was* an artist, or a student one at least. There was something else that for a moment Kate couldn't recall but she felt could be relevant... She read back over her notes and found her interview with Finian Hobbsley, the art gallery owner. Mae had done some work experience there, as had Johnny Papmier... Could Saskia have possibly had any connection with the gallery? Or with Finian Hobbsley, who Mae had apparently found a bit of a creep?

Frustrated, Kate pushed away the folders with enough force to make Chloe look up in surprise.

"You okay? Babies hurting you?"

Kate's hand went automatically to her bump. "No, no they're quiet at the moment, thankfully. It's not them, it's me—"

"How do you mean?"

"Oh, nothing. Just annoyed at how stuck we seem to be on everything..."

Chloe laughed out loud. "Kate, have you *been* a detective long?"

"No, you're right. I know you're right."

"Have a break," said Chloe, her attention returning to her desk.

Thinking this was a good idea, Kate heaved herself and went to fetch herself a glass of water. She took it over to the window nearest the kitchen and looked out at the vista of Abbeyford beneath her. It was a grey, cold, blustery day, which probably wasn't helping her mood. A cherry tree over in the little park across the road was making a brave showing of some pink and white blossom, and a few early daffodils were nodding their bright yellow heads in the breeze, but for all that, it was not an inviting prospect.

Kate sighed to herself. The trouble was, as well, is that she was just getting too tired to really concentrate properly on work. What was even more alarming is that she didn't really *want* to do her job, not right at the moment. She wanted to be at home, in her own house, reading or snoozing on the sofa. A cosy throw covering her, a fire in the wood-burner. Although the absence of Merlin would be a permanent ache...

Come on, woman. Get a grip. That poor girl is out there somewhere, dead or alive and she needs to be found. The longer Mae was missing the more Kate knew that the hope of finding her alive and unharmed was diminishing rapidly. The woman was probably dead anyway, being realistic. But then where was the body?

The sipping of her water and watching the spring flowers had calmed Kate a little, but now she could feel frustration returning. She looked across at Olbeck's office, thinking that she could at least sit down with her friend and thrash this out a little but, of course, he was still absent. Kate went back to her desk to check her phone, but she could see from WhatsApp that he hadn't even read her message yet. *Bugger*.

She sat down and pulled Mae's folder back towards her. Dig into those arty things, perhaps... see if she could find any connections. She turned herself to face her computer screen, brought up an internet browser, and began typing, hoping the impetus of her actions would inspire her to do more.

Olbeck didn't text back until Kate was preparing to leave the office. *So sorry, was out all day with social worker follow up for the kids*. Kate felt a pang of guilt that she hadn't even known this. Luckily his follow up text was *All good so relieved. In office tomorrow so let's catch up then XXXX*. Kate contemplated dropping in on him on her way home but decided against it. No doubt after a day of red tape and bureaucracy, he and Jeff would need a quiet night to themselves and the children.

Slowly, Kate shut down her computer and picked up her coat and bag. She felt a reluctance to leave the office, which was odd as she was once more alone, everyone else having left. Perhaps it was because she felt like she'd achieved absolutely nothing that day. Even odder, she felt a similar reluctance to go home, despite her earlier thoughts. She put her notes away in her bag and pulled on her coat. Maybe she'd go somewhere for a drink for an hour, a bit of time to herself to think and relax. Yes, that's what she would do. She remembered the little pub she'd been to once, on the other side of town. The Something Flowers, wasn't it? She remembered that being a nice, calm place to reflect for an hour or so. She called up a taxi, an extravagance she didn't normally indulge in but there was no way she was walking a couple of miles in her condition.

As she walked in, she saw that the pub was just as she remembered it. Dim lighting, the smell of woodsmoke from the fire in the massive, medieval grate (it was ridiculous really, the pub was ancient and tiny, but the fire dominated it completely). There was a hum of quiet conversation from the few people in there with her.

Kate ordered a drink and found a quiet corner

to sit in, pulling out her notebook once again. She flipped through the pages, finding the mind map she'd begun earlier. *Art gallery* led to *work experience* led to *art tutor*. *Mark Gregory* led to *Mae Denton* led to *Geraint Winner*. *Geraint* led to *Johnny Papmier*, where Kate had underlined his name and written a question mark...

Beside Mae's name, Kate had also written the title of her artwork in the reception area of Abbeyford College. *Secret Place*. What had Chloe said? *There's something funny going on at that college if you ask me...*

Slowly, Kate underlined *Secret Place*. What secrets were being kept, and by whom? Because she knew there *were* secrets. But how was she going to uncover them?

She stared at the notebook once more and then flipped it closed. Her gaze was drawn to the glowing depths of the fire. Kate sighed and picked up her lemonade and sipped it, wishing it were wine.

Chapter Nineteen

"I've been thinking," were the first words that Anderton said to Kate the next morning. He was lying behind her, his hand resting on her bump. One twin stirred lazily under the warmth of his palm.

"That sounds ominous," murmured Kate. She was still sleepy, caught in that hopeful place between wakefulness and unconsciousness, where if the sleeper is lucky, they'll be able to drift back off into slumber. Anderton's words jolted her out of this, slightly to her annoyance. As usual, she hadn't slept well and as it was her day off, she wanted a proper lie in.

"No, seriously. It's been on my mind for a while."

Abandoning the hope of getting more sleep, Kate turned over, with some effort. "What's wrong?"

Anderton brushed her hair away from her face. "Nothing's wrong. I've just been thinking. About the babies and the birth and everything like that."

That *did* sound ominous, to Kate's now wide-awake mind. "What do you mean?"

"Well—"

"You aren't trying to back out of being at the birth, are you?"

For a moment, Anderton looked as though he was going to admit to just that. Then he laughed. "No, of course not. But it did make me think, the scan I mean – and I realise I probably shouldn't say this to a pregnant woman – but what if something went wrong?"

Kate stared at him. She heaved herself up to a sitting position, pulling the duvet up. The central heating didn't automatically come on now it was warmer, and the bedroom was a little chilly. "Wrong?"

"You know, Kate. Birth is – unpredictable. Twin birth doubly – ha – so."

"Well, what do you expect me to do about it?" Kate could hear her voice begin to sharpen. What the hell was Anderton on about?

"It's fine, I wasn't saying – look, I've just been thinking about it – and the fact that we're not married yet and so I wouldn't necessarily be your next of kin—"

"What?" *I need coffee before I have this conversation*, thought Kate.

"I'm not entirely sure what the legality is – who'd have thought I used to be a copper, eh? But I was thinking about it—"

Kate was beginning to get properly annoyed by now. Anderton wasn't normally this waffly. "What the bloody hell are you going on about, Selwyn?"

The rare use of his rare first name alerted Anderton to Kate's wrath. He stopped talking, took a deep breath, sighed, smiled and said, "I was just wondering if you'd like to get married. Really soon. As quickly as possible."

Kate had not been expecting that. She felt herself begin a rapid blinking. Of course, she and Anderton were formally engaged, had been formally engaged for a while, but somehow wedding plans, although discussed at length, had fallen by the wayside. Trampled over by the far more pressing issues of the twins and the absorbing nature of Kate's work. Anderton's too, come to think of it, thought Kate.

Her annoyance subsided. She smiled back at him. "How quickly are we talking? Like, *today*?"

Anderton laughed. "Well, *I* would if we could but unfortunately it takes almost a month. You have to give notice first, things like that."

"Right." Kate pondered for a second. She couldn't see any reason why not and said so.

"Well, it *is* one of the reasons I've been worrying about it, because, you know, we won't really be able to have a big 'do', you know. A big celebration. I highly doubt we'd be able to book anywhere, for a start. And then there's invitations and so forth…"

"You have been thinking this through, haven't you?"

"Of course." He looked at her steadily. "I love you, Kate. I want to marry you."

Touched, Kate squeezed his hand. "Sentiments most definitely returned."

"The thing is, I know I've been married before—"

"I'm glad you're aware of that," said Kate, grinning.

"Ha ha. Anyway, my point is that I've *had* the big wedding. I don't want to deprive you of that, if that's what you want."

Again, Kate pondered. Did she want a big wedding? That would mean they would have to wait until after the twins were born. Which negated the whole point of this conversation. Besides, she suddenly realised, she didn't want a big wedding. She'd never been one for being the centre of attention. In fact, she wasn't so sure that it wasn't something she actually disliked.

She squeezed Anderton's hand again. "I *don't* want a big wedding."

"Honestly?"

"Honestly."

Anderton visibly relaxed. "Well, that's marvellous. We can go on right ahead then!"

Kate started giggling. "What do we do, then, run off to Gretna Green?"

"Would you like to?"

Kate's giggles became a proper laugh. "God, I don't know. Is that even a thing anymore?"

"Of course it is," Anderton said, beginning to laugh himself. "But we don't have to go that far if you don't want to. Abbeyford Registry office is open for business too."

"Well, I don't fancy a trek to Scotland in my condition, to be honest." Kate had no idea where the Abbeyford registry office was and said so. "I'll have a look out for it when I go to work."

"It's actually very pretty. It's in the Old Town, near the square."

Kate thought further. "What about people? How many can we invite?"

Anderton shrugged. "Now that, I don't actually know. But I can find out." He started laughing again. "Unless we go the whole hog and just drag two people in off the street to be our witnesses."

Kate hadn't realised weddings could be *that* small. But there was something rather appealing about the idea. Just her and Anderton and the two babies attending in utero, just their family. But then, wouldn't it be nice to have a loved one or two there as well, to witness the joining of their partnership?

"How about we ask Chloe and Mark to be our witnesses?"

It was Anderton's turn to ponder, but he looked pleased. "Chloe and Mark? Yes, yes, perfect. I would love that, just the four of us."

"Six of us," said Kate, patting her bump.

"Of course, of course. That's who we're going through this for, after all."

"Oi," said Kate, feigning annoyance. "I thought it was because you were madly in love with me."

"That too, of course," said Anderton, grinning.

Kate sat back, thinking about it all. Now that she had pictured it, she was thrilled with the idea – and somehow comforted by it. She said nothing, but reached for her fiancé, holding him close.

Chapter Twenty

KATE COULD HARDLY WAIT FOR the working week to come round again. Although she could have called or texted both Chloe and Olbeck the news, she wanted to ask both in person.

She was therefore a little annoyed to find that Chloe was off for the day and Olbeck was, naturally, in a meeting when she got back to the office. She didn't want to tell anyone else before she asked her two closest friends, not least because she could foresee some offended reactions from those who weren't being asked to be witnesses. She could *hear* Theo's sniffy remark in her head, even as she sat down to her desk.

After a moment's thought, she texted Chloe her news and her request. Plenty of emojis in that message, that was for sure. Kate even added, *sorry, wanted to tell you in person bird but needs must xxx*

Chloe's reply, in the ecstatic affirmative, pinged back mere moments later. She'd put so many love-heart emojis in the message it was difficult to read her words. Kate smiled, touched, and texted back her thanks and appreciation.

There was a moment where Kate could see that Chloe was typing and then a picture shot back, an image of a shotgun. Kate laughed out loud before putting her phone away.

"What's so funny?" asked Theo, who had just come into the office.

"Nothing. Just banter."

"Ha. Well. You look like you're having twins!"

Kate debated getting up from her chair to batter him but couldn't be bothered. She contented herself with a look and turned to her computer, just as the phone rang.

Despite her good mood, she felt a qualm as she went to pick up the receiver. Would this be the call announcing the discovery of Mae Denton's body? *Please no*. She cleared her throat and answered the call.

It was a boy's voice on the end of the line, a rather high, diffident voice. He introduced himself as Geraint Winner.

That name was unusual enough for Kate to be able to immediately place him. No need for her usual method of breezily pretending she knew who the caller was, whilst frantically trawling her memory for their name. Geraint Winner was the young student at Abbeyford whose friendship with Mae was seemingly unknown to her other friends.

Kate kept her voice steady. "What can I help you with, Mr Winner?"

There was a startled pause at the end of the line, as if the young man was unused to being addressed with a title. "Oh – Oh, I mean, I just wanted to talk to someone about Mae. Mae Denton. That's all."

His voice was growing more hesitant by the word. Kate softened her own voice. "Well, you're through to the right place." She introduced herself. "Now, how can we help you? You have something to tell us about Mae?"

She could hear the hesitation on the end of the line. Surely to God, this wasn't going to be a confession? Absurdly, because it was so unlikely, Kate felt her heart rate begin to speed up and one of the twins kicked her in protest.

"Ouch – I mean, sorry, Mr Winner, what was it that you wanted to say?"

Now she could hear the tremble in his voice. "Well, I don't know if it's important – but – but I saw this thing on the news, I mean, with her parents and—" Geraint stopped talking abruptly as the tremble in his voice increased.

Kate broke in. "That's okay, Mr Winner. Is it okay if I call you Geraint?" She took his silence as agreement. "Listen, would it be easier if you came to the station, and we could meet face to face?" Immediately she'd made the suggestion, she thought better. If Geraint was nervous now on the telephone, the noisy station with its slamming doors and possibility of altercations at the booking-in desk was not going to help matters. "Tell you what, how would it be if I came to you? Where would be a good place?"

Geraint sounded less upset but still nervous. "I don't know – I'm supposed to be at college but – well, I bunked off."

"So, are you at home now?"

"No, I'm – well, I'm in the woods. You know, near the college."

The woods near the college – and the quarry. Kate frowned, thinking fast. Young he might be, but she didn't relish a meeting in such an isolated area. Especially in her condition, and with what could be a potential suspect. She thought fast and suggested a café on the high street, being unsure of whether Geraint was old enough to be drinking in pubs. He sounded happy enough with this arrangement and Kate promised she would see him there in half an hour.

Kate looked across at Olbeck's office, still empty of her potential wedding ceremony witness. Oh well, it would have to wait. She wondered what it was that Geraint had to say. Surely if it were something huge – like a confession – he would have sounded a great deal more upset? Oh, he wasn't going to confess, that was wishful thinking. He'd mentioned something about Mae's parents... Perhaps he knew something about the family that the police didn't? Perhaps Mae had confided in him as she hadn't confided in her friends. This was all pure speculation and Kate knew it.

She packed her notebook and accompaniments in

her handbag, thinking of logistics. The café she'd suggested was a ten-minute walk from the police station and, in unpregnant times, Kate would have trotted off there by foot without a second thought. Now, she was seriously contemplating driving the short distance. How different it was when you couldn't rely on your own body anymore, she thought, rather grimly. She imagined for a moment of what it was going to be like; manoeuvring two babies around the town, heaving them in and out of her car, trying to get a double buggy through narrow doors of shops and restaurants. Not that she'd be eating out a great deal once the twins were here, no doubt... It would be a whole new existence, that was for sure...

She decided against her car, purely because the parking in central Abbeyford was a complete bitch, to put it frankly. The ancient town had never been built for motor vehicles. Kate set her teeth and started off, walking slowly to ease the ache in her back. The day had threatened rain beforehand, but luck was with her that morning and the sun was struggling through the dark grey clouds.

The café she had suggested had once been called *Molly's*. It had been styled like an old-fashioned tea shop, the waitresses dressed in forties-style dresses and the whole atmosphere very chintzy and flowery. Now, its name was the rather more modern *Java Junction*. Molly's roses in glass vases and gingham tablecloths had been replaced by an interior that looked like a cross between a coffee factory and a wooden shed. Black pipes crossed the ceiling. Below, they were reflected in the gigantic gleaming espresso machine that dominated the wide wooden bar. Black slate menus were hung on the walls behind it, boasting an impressive range of coffees, as well as teas, smoothies, wraps and pastries. Inevitably, the cups and utensils here were 'fully compostable' and there was mention of all the coffee grounds used being repurposed as fertiliser for the local parks. All very commendable of course, but Kate found herself inwardly casting up her eyes just the same.

Kate looked about her. The coffee shop was fairly empty, the morning rush of office workers long over. She spotted a pale young man in one of the black leather armchairs at the back of the room, next to the noticeboard which advertised a latte art workshop, whatever that was.

"Hello, are you Geraint?"

He looked up and nodded, nervously. He was as lanky and pale as a plant grown in darkness, struggling towards the light. Kate knew he must be at least sixteen to be a student at the college, but he looked younger, almost like a young boy. He reminded her of someone too; someone famous, young and pale with a cap of cropped bleached hair, a face both babyish and angular at the same time. Kate took the matching armchair facing the one occupied by Geraint, and sat down with relief.

"Could I get you a drink?" She asked it just for something to say as she could see he still had a half full cup of something green and foamy in front of him. Even as he shook his head with a muttered *thanks*, she was wishing she could have one of the drinks up on the board. Pretentious this place might be, but damn, the coffee smelt good.

Kate was opening her mouth to begin with a few small-talk remarks to put Geraint at his ease but as she did, he leant forward.

"I've got to tell you something about Mae – I don't think the police know and I don't think anyone else does either."

Kate held her pen poised by her notebook. "That's fine, Geraint. You can tell me."

He seemed to hesitate for a moment, as if thinking better of his decision. Eminem, Kate thought, with faint amusement. A young Eminem, that's who he looks like.

"Mae and I were friends, good friends." Geraint held Kate's gaze almost defiantly, as if expecting her to protest.

"Yes, I've heard that."

Geraint looked away. "She – I – She wanted me to keep it a secret – said it would be awful if anyone found out."

"Yes," said Kate. *Get on with it, lad.*

Geraint took a deep breath. "She was having an affair with one of the teachers. At the college." He said it in a rush of breath, and then sat back in his chair, looking away.

"I see." Kate made a note. "Who is the teacher?"

"I don't know." Kate caught his eye again with a meaningful look and Geraint blushed, a tide of pink blooming on his pale face. "I mean – well – it's Mr Gregory."

Mae's art teacher. I *see*, thought Kate. Was Geraint telling the truth? And if he was, what did it mean for the investigation?

Geraint was looking both relieved and uneasy at the same time. He can't be more than seventeen, thought Kate, with a touch of compassion. She leant forward as much as she could over her bump.

"Thank you for telling me, Geraint. Can I just ask though, before we go into what you've just said, what made you tell me – us – now? I know that Mae had asked you to keep it a secret and you have, up until now. So, what made you change your mind?"

The blush had faded now, but his expression had darkened. He didn't answer her for a moment, looking out of the plate-glass window at the side of the room, which had replaced the whimsical many-barred windows of Molly's.

"I saw this interview," he said, with difficulty. "With her parents."

He stopped speaking again. After a moment, Kate prompted, thinking of Tin, "In the paper?"

"No, on TV. They had an interview with them, just

on the news I think or something like that, and they just, they were so upset—" He stopped talking again and returned his gaze to the window.

"I see," said Kate, as gently as she could. "I understand. Well, let's just sit back for a moment and then we can talk. You can tell me all about it."

Geraint cleared his throat. "As much as I know."

"Yes, as much as you know. It can only help."

Chapter Twenty-One

THE ROOM LOOKED LIKE AN art gallery. That was the only way to describe it, Mae thought, and she'd thought that from the start. It was a prison, *her* prison, a cell, with no windows and a locked door, but it was also a gallery. High ceilings and pristine white walls would have provided the perfect backdrop for artwork on display, but there was no artwork. There was only her.

There were no paintings, no sculpture, no ceramics. There were spotlights on the ceiling trained onto parts of the wall but with no artwork to be illuminated. The circles of light were stationary, but Mae could make them move, swaying her head a little, or squinting her eyes. It was something to do.

The floor was tiled in black and white like a chessboard and highly polished. The only furniture in the room was her – she was thinking of it as hers by now – her chaise longue. That and the chain that bound her wrist were the only other things in the room, apart from herself.

Sometimes he came and took her to another room,

a tiny room with a sink and a toilet, where she would be ordered to bathe and relieve herself. This happened regularly but not so regularly that she could make any sort of plan that might involve her escape. There was nothing in the bathroom – it wasn't an actual bathroom but she didn't know what else to call it – but the sink and the toilet. The sink was made out of one piece of shiny white porcelain and the toilet was likewise.

Mae remembered her dad had once showed her the cistern of the toilet at home, by taking off the top of the toilet. Inside was its plumbing ball and metal rod that was attached to it. That would have been good; that would have been a weapon. But here, the cistern was unreachable without pulling the whole toilet away from the wall. And even if Mae had the strength to do that – she was getting weaker, she knew that – that was a course of action she couldn't contemplate, given what would no doubt happen when he found out. No, she wouldn't do that, not yet. She wasn't – yet – that desperate.

She didn't know why she was being held as this – this *exhibit*. She was fed and watered; good food, as far as she could tell, although not much of it. Always on paper plates, which he would take away again afterwards. Always food that could be eaten with her fingers, no cutlery provided. The water came in a plastic bottle and he took that away too, once she'd drunk.

Apart from the first time, when she'd had to pose for him and he'd taken photographs, he hadn't touched her. She'd tried talking to him but apart from one time, he had simply ignored her.

The one time, when she had asked, trying to keep the tears from her voice, why she was there, he'd said "Purity, that's why. You need to be purified. You're not quite ready yet."

"Ready for what?"

He'd shaken his head then, backed from the room and locked the door.

Mae was growing confused as to time. How long had she been here? There were some days when she wondered whether she was actually here at all, in this strange room. Had she died, up at the quarry? She could remember nothing other than a dark shape, a movement in the blackness and then – nothing. Nothing until she woke up here.

If I'm not dead, then I have to try and escape. Mae drew her legs up to her chest and hugged herself, slippery silk under her bare arms. The chain dragged at her wrist. *I must escape.* But how?

Chapter Twenty-Two

Unwilling to risk Olbeck being trapped in another meeting when she got back from interviewing Geraint, Kate called him as she walked back to the office.

"Oh, really?" were his words on hearing the news. "That sounds promising."

"Are you in the office?"

"For the next fifteen minutes. Then I've got to go. Got a—"

"Meeting," Kate finished for him. She walked faster, trying not to wince at the ache in the tendons of her groin. "Can you please just try and wait for me just so I can quickly go over this with you?"

"Yes. Where are you? You sound out of breath."

Kate had rounded the corner of the road to the station. "I'll be five minutes," she puffed. "Just stay there."

"You numpty, you're scarlet in the face," said Olbeck, when she finally gasped her way into his office. "You're supposed to be taking it easy. I would have waited for you!"

"I know." Kate fell thankfully into the chair that he pulled out for her, and they both laughed at the alarming creak it gave out as her weight settled into it. "God, this thing better hold."

"Just stay still," said Olbeck, half amused, half anxious. "I don't think I could get you off the floor..."

"Oh, *cheers*." Kate tried to get her breathing under control. "Just give me a moment..."

Olbeck fetched her a glass of water and she sipped between gasps for air.

"Jeff doesn't know how lucky he is," she said, when she could speak. "*He* didn't have to go through this to get your two." Immediately she said this, she regretted it. It wasn't as if Olbeck and Jeff's route to parenthood had been exactly easy. "Sorry. No offence."

Olbeck waved a hand. "None taken. Anyway, Geraint Winner?"

Kate reached for her notebook. "Yes. Like I said, he said that Mae Denton and Mark Gregory had been having an affair. He's – Gregory, I mean – is Mae's art teacher."

"I thought I recognised the name. Dirty dog." Olbeck raised his eyebrows. "That's if it's true."

"Oh, I think it is. He had pictures. Geraint, I mean."

"What?"

Kate giggled, although it wasn't really funny. "He showed them to me. Clear pictures of Mae and Gregory in a clinch."

"Really?" Olbeck sat back in his chair. There was a moment's silence. "Does anything about that strike you as odd?"

"Um – most of it?"

They exchanged a glance. "Right," Olbeck went on. "So, Geraint and Mae are friends, right?"

"According to him."

"So, if you came across your friend in a steamy clinch with a teacher, *their* teacher, is your first reaction to take photos of it?"

They looked at each other again. "You know, it might be," admitted Kate. "These young 'uns live their lives in front of a camera – and behind one too."

"I suppose so." Olbeck rubbed his jaw. "What else did he say?"

Kate scanned her notes. "Just that Mae said it had been going on for a while, but he had to keep it a secret because Mark Gregory is married—"

"Of course - and her teacher... What *is* the legality of that, by the way? I mean, she's technically not a child..."

"I'm not sure. Legally, I think he's in the clear, Gregory, I mean, but morally – it's pretty sordid if you think about it, isn't it?"

Olbeck nodded. "Anything else?"

"They used to meet in the quarry. It was their secret place, apparently." Kate thought of the painting Mae had named exactly that. How had Mark Gregory felt, seeing that every day in the college reception, knowing what he knew? Was it part of the thrill to have it so openly displayed? She remembered he'd lied about knowing it was there. Well, he would, wouldn't he?

Olbeck's eyebrows had gone up again. "The quarry? Right – so he could well be the person Mae was going to meet when she disappeared. I *see*."

"What do you want me to do?"

"I want Gregory brought in immediately. Under caution if necessary, but not if he's going to come quietly." Olbeck paused for a moment and said, with delicacy. "I think Rav and Theo should take that job."

Normally, Kate would have protested, but she saw his point. "Okay. What else?"

"I think Mae's other friends should be reinterviewed." Olbeck threw his hands up in the air. "*Again*. Certainly Johnny Papmier and the other friend, what's-her-name, Lucy. If Geraint knew about the affair, did they? And if they did, why the hell haven't they said?"

"Chloe and I will cover that." Kate flipped her notebook closed, pleased that there was a plan of action.

"Why did Geraint come out with this all, by the way?"

Kate thought back. "Apparently, he saw some interview with her parents on the TV. It appealed to his conscience."

"Hmm." Olbeck and Kate exchanged another glance. "Well, that might be the case, but we'll have to see."

"Right." Kate paused for a moment, gathering the energy to get up. Then she remembered what she had to ask her old friend. The excitement of the last few hours had driven it from her head. "Oh, by the way, Anderton and I are getting married. Do you fancy coming?" She was rewarded by his genuine double-take and started laughing. "Well, do you?"

"What the hell – of course I'll be coming. But – what – I didn't know you'd made any arrangements? When is it? *Where* is it?"

Still chuckling, Kate revealed the plan, asking him to be one of the witnesses. She was half pleased and half alarmed to see tears in his eyes as she told him.

Olbeck got up to hug her. "Of course I will. Of course." She was so large that he could barely get his arms around her, but he gave it his best shot. "What a wonderful surprise. Is it literally going to be the four of us?"

"Yes. Not even Jeff, sorry. Not until afterwards."

"He'll have to watch the kids, anyway. Oh, congratulations, darling. I'm really thrilled for you."

Kate squeezed him back. "Thank you."

Olbeck released her. "I'll look out my tux. What fun!"

Kate laughed again. "Well, quite. Not exactly textbook but that's how we roll."

They both laughed. "Right, you," said Olbeck, going back to his chair. "Enough of the fun stuff. Let's get back to work."

Chapter Twenty-Three

CHLOE WAS OUT OF THE office, so Kate made the phone calls to Johnny Papmier and Lucy Atkins herself, arranging them for the next day. Chloe and Kate worked well together, their rapport and empathy better than Kate had found with interviewing with her other colleagues. Of course, it hadn't always been like that...

Chloe picked Kate up the next morning in her sporty little car, a far cry from the old bangers that she once had. Sitting beside Chloe in the passenger seat as they sped out of Abbeyford, Kate chuckled, more than a few memories surfacing.

"What's so funny?"

"I was just thinking of when we first met."

Chloe began to grin. "Oh. Yeah. Wasn't the *best* start in the world, was it, bird?"

"Nope. Still, things have improved."

Chloe gave her an affectionate glance. There was a comfortable silence until she added, "God, that seems like a long time ago."

"I know." Kate thought back to that case; the body

of the young man at Muddiford Beach, his bare feet washed by the tide. How Chloe had despised her, the first time they'd met! Thinking of that time brought back the memory of Tin ambushing her with a microphone and a cameraman, just as they came off the scene. *Dickhead.* As if Chloe had read her mind, her friend mentioned the 'date' she'd had with him the other night.

"Do you think that's why Anderton popped the question?" Chloe said, grinning. "Did he get jealous and think that Tin was about to steal you away?"

"Hardly." Kate and Chloe had discussed the new wedding plans in detail, but Kate didn't want to go into exactly why she and Anderton wanted to make their relationship a formality. Almost unconsciously, her hands went to the mound of her stomach, bulging through the straps of the seatbelt.

"Remember when you were going to go to New York with Tin, and I gave you a bollocking about it?"

"What is this, a drive down Memory Lane? And you didn't give me a bollocking."

"I did, a bit."

"You *advised* me," said Kate with a smile. "And anyway, you were quite right. Lucky I took your advice, wasn't it?"

Chloe laughed. "Well, things generally turn out for the best." A shadow crossed her face as she said it, and Kate wondered whether she was thinking of Roman, poor lost Roman, who'd died in such a horrible way.

Still, Chloe was better now, indubitably better. Whether that was due to time, Chloe's own robust efforts in healing herself, or the addition of Carl Lopez to her life, Kate was unsure, but she was very glad about it all the same.

Mae's best female friend Lucy lived outside of Abbeyford, in the small pretty village of Cudston Magma. The house owned by (Kate assumed) Lucy's parents could have sprung fully formed from the pages of an Agatha Christie novel. A cottage made of mellow red bricks, hung with ivy and wisteria, its tendrils dry and brown at this time of year. A trio of rosebushes stood in the tiny front garden, minute green shoots just visible on their thorny stems.

"Lovely," said Kate, heaving herself from the car.

"Bit boring round here for a teenager, don't you think?" Chloe looked around at the pastoral scene, undeniably charming but very quiet and unspoilt.

"Maybe—" began Kate but by then the front door to the cottage had opened.

Kate hadn't spoken to Lucy before. She was a pretty girl, tall (why were all these youngsters so *tall*?), with a long sweep of blonde hair carefully waved and styled. Thankfully – to Kate's mind – Lucy had resisted the lure of eyebrows like furry slugs, and thick stripes of contouring make-up ruining – in Kate's mind – her beautiful young face.

Don't I sound like an old fart, thought Kate as she and Chloe greeted the girl and held out their identification. I wonder if I'm having a girl – or two girls even, Anderton's insistence on a penis notwithstanding? What will they be wearing or looking like, in eighteen years' time? Full-face metal masks? Demon horns? Additional ears grafted to the sides of their heads?

Let's get there first, Kate. Shaking off these ridiculous notions, Kate followed Lucy and Chloe into the interior of the cottage. Short – petite, thank you – as Kate was, even she found she had to duck her head as they made their way to the rear of the building, down a single step into the kitchen.

This had been extended at the back. Large windows looked onto a very lovely English cottage garden, not looking its best at this time of year but showing the promise of Spring glory to come. Bright daffodils clustered beneath an old, ivy-hung wall and, as Kate watched, a black and white cat sauntered across the small lawn before jumping up to the top of the opposite wall. The memory of Merlin gave her a sharp pang.

"Would you – would you like coffee? Or something?" Lucy's voice was high and clear and unmistakeably middle-class.

"That would be lovely, thanks Lucy." Chloe made herself at home at the bleached oak kitchen table. Kate eased herself down onto one of the chairs without saying anything.

Lucy busied herself with the kettle. She was nervous, Kate could tell that even by looking at her turned back. At one point, she fumbled getting a mug from one of the cupboards and it fell to the kitchen counter, fortunately not breaking. But that didn't mean anything. For all Lucy knew, the two police officers were coming to tell her that they'd found Mae's body.

As Lucy put the mugs on the table, overfull and slopping steaming brown liquid onto the clean wood of the surface, Kate gave Chloe an expressive glance. She'd already said she would be taking a back seat in this interview. She wanted to observe more than anything, not having talked to Lucy before.

"Please don't worry, Lucy," Chloe said. "We've not come with bad news. Or good news, either, unfortunately."

Lucy nodded, bunching up her mouth. The skin of her face was soft, almost translucent, her cheeks still babyishly rounded – but for all that and the blonde hair and the willowy look, Kate sensed a toughness about her, a core of steel.

Even so, Lucy had tears in her eyes. "What was it you wanted?"

"Some new information has come to us, about Mae, I mean. I'm just going to ask you straight out – were you aware that she was having an affair with her art tutor, Mr Mark Gregory?"

The effect was immediate. The milky skin flushed straight up, and Lucy's eyes widened. Kate was reminded of Geraint's blush, but there was something there besides the shock in Lucy's face. After a moment, Kate placed it. It was anger.

"*What?*"

Chloe repeated her sentence, and added, "Did you know?"

"Me?" Lucy's voice had become shrill rather than high. "No, I fucking *didn't*." She made no apology for her language. She was blinking rapidly, and from this, and her general demeanour, Kate thought she was probably telling the truth.

The two officers waited. Lucy jumped up, upsetting one of the cups completely (fortunately, Kate had drunk most of its contents already). She took no notice of the small pool of coffee spreading on the table but walked to the half-glassed back door, pressing her hands against it.

"I'm sorry if this has upset you," said Chloe, glancing at Kate. "You really didn't know?"

"No. I had no idea – I didn't—" Lucy turned to face them and then swung back towards the garden. Within it, the black and white cat was crossing back over the lawn. There was a moment's silence and then both women heard her say *fuck* very slowly and quietly.

"Lucy, would you sit down again please? We do need to talk to you about this."

Kate, waiting for the girl to obey Chloe's command, thought she should find a cloth or something and wipe up the table. Trouble was, she seemed to have wedged herself somewhat firmly between the chair and the table, and consequently couldn't move. She eyed the brown liquid as it crept towards her.

Lucy, turning back to the room, made a tutting noise and grabbed some kitchen roll. Wiping up the spill, she sat down again, seemingly more under control of her emotions. The three women regarded each other over the table for a moment.

"Sorry about that," said Lucy, her voice a little ragged. "It was just – I really did have no idea. I was just so shocked that Mae wouldn't – didn't—" Tears rose in her eyes once more and she glanced away. "I'm beginning to think I didn't know her at all."

"It must be upsetting," soothed Chloe. "Particularly in light of her continued disappearance."

"Yes." Lucy blinked and looked away. "I really miss her. I wake up every morning, you know, and for a moment I can't believe it, I don't remember. Just for a split second." She looked at Kate and Chloe and there was real fear in her eyes. "I just keep thinking, if we don't find her, if you don't find her – I don't mean find her alive, I think—" Her voice clogged completely at this moment, and she stopped talking and cleared her throat. "I mean, if she's not found in – in any way, then I might be like this for the rest of my life. You know, waking up every morning, having to go through it again."

"I'm so sorry," said Chloe. "I know it's particularly

hard for you and Johnny as you were such close friends of hers."

"Yes, we were. Are, I mean."

"What about Geraint Winner? He was the one who told us about the affair."

Blood rushed up into Lucy's face again. "Geraint? How did he know about it?" Anger infused her face again. "Why would she tell him and not me?"

That was a puzzle Kate had been trying to solve, too. She spoke up for the first time. "We're wondering about Mae's friendship with Geraint, Lucy. When we first spoke to you and Johnny and Mae's other friends about him, it seemed as if you didn't really know that they were at all – involved, shall we say? As friends, I mean."

Lucy looked away. "We didn't really know. That's what I mean about Mae keeping secrets, about not telling me stuff. That's what I mean about me not really knowing her at all." A note of curiosity crept into her voice. "How long – I mean, the affair with Mr Gregory – is that really true?"

"We believe so."

"What has he – I mean, Mr Gregory – said about it?"

Chloe smiled at her to take the sting from her words. "I'm afraid we can't talk about that with you at the moment, Lucy." She paused for a moment before steering the conversation back to where she wanted it to be. Kate gave her a silent nod of approval. "Let's talk about Geraint, shall we? You say you and Mae's other friends weren't aware of her and him being... close?"

Lucy looked sulky. "I don't know – Mae never really mentioned him. He's a creep anyway, a right little suck-up."

Chloe looked interested. "Oh, really?"

Lucy nodded. "He just smarms around, trying to get in with anyone he thinks might be, oh, I don't know – useful to him. Mae felt sorry for him, I think. He's gay, you know, right?" She looked at Chloe and then at Kate. "Why that would make her feel sorry for him, I don't know, but that's what she said one day to me in the canteen. Just commented on how he seemed to be on his own a lot, that he must be lonely."

"Because he was gay? Surely he can't be the only gay person at college, Lucy?"

"That's what *I* said. In fact, I know he's not. Anyway, she didn't say much more about him."

"So, you weren't aware she was spending so much time with him?"

The sulky look was back. "Mae was – well, she was often up to stuff I didn't know about, I mean, she wasn't constantly *available*, you know." Anger flickered again. "Right, and now I know *why*."

Her voice broke once more and Lucy looked away, back out into the garden.

Chapter Twenty-Four

"What did you think?" Kate asked Chloe as they drove their way home.

"Don't know, really. Didn't you think there was a lot of anger there? At Mae, I mean?"

Kate eased the seatbelt from her stomach. "Yes. I thought that, exactly."

"Might not mean anything." Chloe flicked the indicator for the Abbeyford road. The sun was shining now and the daffodils on the verge dipped and swayed their yellow heads in the strong wind that buffeted the car. "You know what teenage girls are like. All the *drama*."

"True." Kate was silent for a moment, going over what they had learnt. Was it anything of significance? Had Rav and Theo discovered anything better?

"Wonder how the boys got on with Gregory?" Chloe mused, articulating Kate's thoughts out loud.

"Mmm." Kate was preoccupied with another sensation, that of nausea rapidly travelling up from her middle.

"You okay?"

Kate thought of pretending she was fine, realised rapidly that she wasn't. "Oh God, Chloe, can you pull over? Think I'm going to be sick."

"Christ." Chloe swung the car into a handy layby and Kate tumbled out, just in time.

After an unpleasant noisy interlude by the back wheel (fortunately shielded from the few cars that were passing), Kate got back in the car, without comment. Also without comment, Chloe passed her a tissue and a half full bottle of water.

"I knew I shouldn't have had that coffee."

"Well, thanks for not puking all over my dashboard." Chloe gave her a sideways glance. "You all right if we keep going?"

"Yes, sure. Sorry. Better now."

Chloe pulled back into the road. "Hey, at least you won't have to worry about this when the babies are actually here."

"Let's hope not." Kate leant back against the passenger seat and closed her eyes. "Sleepless nights, shitty nappies and bleeding nipples, yes, but Exorcist-style vomiting, no. Let us look on the bright side."

Theo and Rav were still out of the office by the time the women got back. Kate, who was actually feeling rather chipper after getting rid of that coffee, typed up her notes from the interview with Lucy Atkins. She and Chloe were interviewing Johnny Papmier that afternoon and, given what they had learned from Mae's female friend, Kate wondered whether Johnny was going to react in a similar fashion. Or would he be angrier? Or had he known?

She looked at her notes. Had Lucy's anger at Mae's deception with Gregory been because of hurt pride that her friend had not confided in her? Or was there something else? Was Mae's relationship with Geraint really of consequence, in terms of the investigation, or was it simply a soft-hearted girl's friendship with a younger boy because she felt sorry for him?

For the first time, Kate made herself confront the possibility that Mae's friends had had something to do with her disappearance. Of course, they had all been suspected in the early days of the investigation (she sighed at the thought that there were 'early days' now) but Lucy and Johnny had never been considered serious suspects. Had Johnny known of Mae's affair with Gregory? Had he been jealous? Jealous enough to kill Mae? Although surely if that was the case then where was the body? Intelligent as these two teenagers were, Kate couldn't believe that they had the experience and the wit to outsmart an entire department of experienced detectives.

She thought back to the suicide cases that she'd seen at the College, all those years ago. She'd been with Tin then but still battling her attraction to Anderton. How times changed. Something that Tin had said recurred to her. Kate flipped back through her notes. *Life model*. She stared into space just as Chloe placed a full water glass by her elbow. Life model.

It was an odd term, wasn't it? As if there were *dead models* out there, too.

"Here, drink this. You're probably still a bit dehydrated."

"Oh, thanks, bird." Kate drank it down, but slowly, feeling the coolness of it all the way down the back of her throat. "I was just thinking about the art connection."

"Yes?"

"I told you, didn't I, that Tin told me that Saskia Devonshire, you know, one of the other missing girls, had been a life model?"

"Did you?" Chloe looked interested. "Think that's something we should be looking into?"

"Yes, I do." Another thought reoccurred to Kate, the stacks of paintings at the gallery in Salterton. The ones that the owner, what was his name – Hobbsley – had joshingly forbidden her to look at. "I think Sea Views needs some more investigation, or at least another visit."

Chloe sat down at her chair opposite Kate and put her elbows on the table, leaning her chin in her hands. "Enlighten me."

"Well, like I said, Tin told me that Saskia Devonshire had done some life modelling. Mae's an artist – well, an art student – and she also did some work experience for the gallery in Salterton. Now, the owner of Sea Views, who, incidentally, Mae thought was a bit of a creep apparently does 'private commissions'"

Kate quirked her two index fingers in the air and went on. "He wouldn't show me the painting and I didn't query it, which I'm a bit surprised about myself to be honest. I just think he's worth another interview."

Chloe looked a bit confused. "Why, do you think he asked Mae to pose for him or something?"

Kate shrugged. "Just an idea. I'm not saying he's done away with her or anything. It's just – now I'm starting to see there might be another connection, that's all."

Chloe pushed her chair back from her desk and jumped up. "Well, I'm all for that, but we've got young Johnny to interview first. Shall I drive again?"

Kate herself got up, as briskly as she could. "Actually, Chloe, you go and see Johnny. I'll take Mr Fancy Pants Hobbsley."

Chloe looked anxious. "You sure?"

"I'm sure. I could do with some sea air."

Kate didn't call ahead to the gallery. Foolish, perhaps, as it was a Tuesday and Kate had found that little independent shops tended to shut on a Tuesday (God knows why Tuesday and not Monday). But she was in the mood to tackle the owner and if he wasn't at the gallery, she would damn well track him down at his home.

The good weather held as she drove towards Salterton although as she approached the coast road, the wind grew so strong that the car actually rocked. Kate had taken a pool car, not having driven in that morning, and although it was a large one, she found the slew of the wheel beneath her palms quite alarming. She was glad when she reached the car park on the front and could get out.

The sea itself was heaving with white horses, the waves whipped and foamy. Sea spray stung her eyes as Kate locked up the car. She had often envied Chloe for living here, not least in the summertime, when the beach was golden and the sea was (relatively) warm. Now, with the sun disappearing behind dark clouds and the wet wind buffeting her, Kate was rather thankful for her cosy inland home.

The gallery was open, which was one win, and Finian Hobbsley was in attendance, a second one. He recognised her as soon as she pushed open the door to the gallery, she could tell. Well, she was kind of hard to miss at the moment. Kate noted the flash of alarm that crossed his face as she closed the door behind her, shoving it against the push of the wind. That expression was almost immediately gone, covered with the twinkle that she'd experienced the first time around.

"Detective Inspector, what a pleasant surprise. How are you? Isn't this weather absolutely *beastly*?"

Kate, pretending that her hair wasn't completely windswept across her damp face, brushed it back with what she hoped was an insouciant hand. "Good afternoon, Mr Hobbsley. No, it's not very nice, is it?"

"What can I do for you?" The strain behind the twinkle was glimpsed again for a moment.

"I have some more questions for you, I'm afraid, Mr Hobbsley."

"Oh dear. Nothing serious, I hope? I assume this is about poor Mae, again?" He waited, obviously hoping that Kate would elaborate but she said nothing, merely smiling at him. There was a moment's silence.

"Could I offer you a coffee, perhaps?"

Kate repressed a shudder. "No, no, no thank you, I'm fine." She spotted a chair against the wall. "I'll have a seat though, if I may."

"Of course, of course." Hobbsley waved her towards it. "Perhaps – perhaps you'd be more comfortable in the back? We could talk more privately in there."

A tingle ran up Kate's spine, a zip of something she'd felt before. "No, no," she said again. "I'm fine here, thanks."

Hobbsley looked discomforted. "Well, then..." For a moment, he stood as if at a loss. "I'll just – I'll just turn the sign to 'closed' then, so we won't be interrupted."

Kate acted on impulse. "Actually, Mr Hobbsley, leave that for now. I will come through to the back, to the stockroom. There's something in particular I'd like you to show me."

The discomfort had given way to frank alarm. "What do you mean?" He added, after a moment, "Inspector?"

Kate smiled at him, partly to put him at his ease, and partly to calm herself. She wasn't sure whether the jitters she was experiencing were because of Hobbsley, or the lingering remnants of the caffeine she'd had this morning, or from some mysterious pregnancy hormonal shift. Whatever happened, she wasn't going to let him lock her in here, that was for sure.

"I'd like you to show me the project you're currently working on," she said.

Hobbsley's eyes widened. "The project..."

"Yes, the one you were making on commission. The one you mentioned last time I was here."

"But – but it's private."

"This is a police investigation, Mr Hobbsley, as I'm sure you're aware."

"Yes. Yes, I know." Hobbsley looked very unhappy. "It's just – it is a private commission. I'm not supposed to show anyone."

"I appreciate that. But I do have to see it."

"Right. Right." The twinkle had completely gone by now. He still made no move to show her.

"Mr Hobbsley?" Kate inclined her head towards the door to the back room .

"Yes. Yes, I'm sorry." He hesitated once more and then asked, "Tell me, do you know much about art, Inspector Redman?"

"Absolutely nothing," said Kate, cheerfully. "I don't even know what I like."

Finian Hobbsley visibly relaxed. "Oh, oh yes – very funny."

"It's true," said Kate. "I'm afraid I know absolutely nothing about it."

The faint glimmer of a twinkle resurfaced in Hobbsley's eyes. "Oh well, you're far from the only one, Inspector. I'm sorry to have kept you waiting. Please do come this way."

He stood aside and gestured for her to go first, into the back room of the gallery.

Chapter Twenty-Five

SHE WAS GETTING WEAKER. MAE knew it, despite the food that was given to her regularly. It was given to her regularly, provided she didn't misbehave. *Misbehave*, that was what he called it. A ladylike word, for ladylike behaviour. Misbehaviour sounded like something a Jane Austen character would do at a ball, behind a curtain, perhaps, or by flirting with a fan. Mae's misbehaviour had been slightly more serious than that.

She'd dug into the chaise longue with her fingernails, ripping the golden silk. It had been partly to see if she could find a nail, a screw, anything with a sharp edge. Only partly. Partly it had been terror and frustration; terror at not knowing what was going to happen to her, locked in this cell, on display for him whenever he wanted. Terror at not knowing when she would be 'pure' enough for him. And when she was pure, then what?

She hadn't found anything sharp. When he'd come back, standing outside the door as usual and told her to put on the blindfold, she'd hesitated for a moment.

The blindfold, a stretchy circle of black fabric, had been left for her not long after she regained consciousness. More than once, Mae had contemplated the elasticity of that fabric. How long would it stretch? Long enough for her to upend the chaise longue and tie it to one of the legs? That would be an escape, that would take her out of here. But to where? And she didn't want to die, she wanted to live. Besides, the chaise longue was bolted to the floor.

So, she'd hesitated, and he'd unlocked the door and seen her uncovered face. But the triumph she'd felt as his face contorted was swiftly dissipated by the blow he gave her to the side of her head. She'd cried out and fallen, the chain tinkling as she fell to the floor. He'd hit her again on her head and leant down and hissed in her ear, so she could hear it even over her sobs.

"It doesn't matter if you see my face, my dear. Not anymore."

He'd said nothing else but gave her one last blow that rocked her head over on one side. Mae thought she must have passed out, because when she came to, the room was dark, and she was stiff and cold from lying on the floor. Slowly, weeping, she'd dragged herself onto the chaise longue and curled into a ball, holding her ringing head and trying to stifle her sobs, as they hurt her more.

She'd starved for three days for that. The only time she saw him was twice a day when he took her to the small room with the toilet. She couldn't help but cringe away from him as he came near her, but he'd laughed and shaken his head, as if he couldn't believe her behaviour. Her *misbehaviour*.

He'd escorted her back to the chaise longue and locked up the chain again. Despite the velvet padding on the inside, her arm had chafed. He tutted when he saw this and stood back and shook his head again.

"It's not the same," he said, regarding her with a touch of – could it be – reproach? "Just not the same. But then Poppy was a one off."

He'd left then and she'd been too weak and hurt and traumatised to pay heed to his words. But now, days later, when she'd been fed once more, Mae remembered. *Poppy was a one off.*

Who was Poppy? Mae lay on her golden bed and thought, as much as she could assemble the fog in her head into something resembling thought. Poppy? Did she know a Poppy?

Someone at college? One of Johnny's girlfriends? Someone she'd worked with at the gallery last year?

Mae knew she'd heard that name before, sometime before, before this nightmare began. But where?

Chapter Twenty-Six

"Did you hear?"

Kate, putting her bag down by her desk, looked across at Chloe in surprise at her tone. "No, what?"

"We've arrested Mark Gregory."

Kate raised her eyebrows. "No. Seriously?"

"Seriously. They interviewed him yesterday, let him go and then apparently when I got in, Rav said they'd been back to arrest him for more questioning."

Kate sat down. "Do the press know?"

"Yep. Only that we've got someone helping with our enquiries at the moment, but I doubt it'll be long before his name's out there."

Kate was silent. If Olbeck had sanctioned the arrest of Mark Gregory, then did that mean that she'd been off on a wild goose chase with her theories about art and its angle to the case? "Hmm. What do you think?"

Chloe shrugged. "Apparently, his alibi for the night of Mae's disappearance has collapsed. You know he said he was home with his wife, right? Well, apparently we've got a witness stating that he was seen near the quarry on the night she went missing."

"Really? Who's the witness?"

"Geraint Winner."

"Again!" Kate exploded. "What's with this kid? Why wouldn't he have told us before?"

"Same reason as he didn't mention the affair in the first place? Got an attack of conscience?"

"Huh." Kate eased her back in the chair, reaching around to rub it. "Seriously, Mark Gregory is considered a serious suspect? As in our number one?"

Chloe shrugged again. "Look, I only know what I've heard. Have a word with Mark, or grab Theo when he comes back from interviewing."

"Right."

Chloe headed off somewhere, leaving Kate staring at the long list of emails she had to deal with and wondering whether she was seriously losing her touch. If Mark Gregory was now the prime suspect, then all her theories about the link between the other missing girls and Mae were all so much rubbish. She tapped her fingers on the edge of the desk, crimping her mouth. The twins, reacting to the tension, roiled and kicked inside her.

Oh, to hell with it. Kate pushed herself up out of her chair and made her way to the door. She'd have a quick peek at the interview with Mark Gregory, up in the viewing room.

The viewing room was part of the IT department.

It was currently staffed by someone Kate vaguely recognised as one of Sam Hollingsworth's new hires, a young woman who looked barely out of her teens. She smiled nervously as Kate explained what she wanted to do. There wasn't much room to sit down, even less so with a pregnant belly and Ayla, the young technician, kindly offered Kate her own seat.

She would have been able to tell the interview wasn't going particularly well, even if the sound hadn't been turned up. Mark Gregory wore a frown of permanent outrage and they had clearly long since hit the 'no comment' stage of the interview. Theo and Rav were giving it their best shot but Kate, veteran of many an interview, could tell they weren't going to be able to glean much from the man's answers.

"So, you're telling us that you were near the quarry on the night of Mae Denton's appearance, but that you had a legitimate reason to be there?"

Mark Gregory glared ahead. "No comment."

"You told us earlier that it was because you had some files you needed to collect from your classroom that evening to take home to mark?"

"No comment."

"Mr Gregory, can you tell us why you lied about your whereabouts beforehand when we asked you for your movements on the night of Mae Denton's disappearance?"

"No comment."

Kate sighed, which made Ayla give her a worried

glance. Kate smiled at her. "Don't worry, Ayla, this is all par for the course, I'm afraid. As you'll find out."

The girl smiled again, a little uncertainly. Kate turned her attention back to the screen.

"You've admitted having an affair with Mae Denton, an affair that you say has been ongoing for several months. Can you say why you hadn't thought to mention this to us before, especially in the light of her disappearance?"

"No comment."

"Was Mae Denton threatening you, Mr Gregory? Did she threaten to tell your wife about the affair?"

Kate could see Gregory clench himself tighter, his whole body like a fist. "No, she – it wasn't—" He appeared to recollect himself. "It wasn't like that." There was a cough and shift of position from the solicitor sitting next to him. "No comment."

"Did you threaten or harm Mae Denton, Mr Gregory? Do you know where she is?"

"No comment."

Kate had had enough. Sometimes, overlooking interviews, she could see where they were going wrong, but she had nothing with which to critique Theo's method this time. He, she and possibly Mark Gregory, could see that this was a pointless endeavour.

She thanked Ayla, squeezed herself and her stomach out of the room and took the lift back down to the office. The Gregory situation was out of her hands, so it made more sense for her to follow up those leads she'd already made a start on. Yes, Mark Gregory obviously had been hiding something of extreme interest to those working the case, but that didn't mean Kate's musings were completely off track, did it? She had that feeling, heightened now, that there was something more to this case, something beneath the surface. Something, infuriatingly, that she had – *seen*? Could that be the word? Was there something about this case that she'd experienced before, or *seen* before – or was it connected to a case that she'd worked before?

When Kate reached this stage of cogitation, she knew she couldn't stay in the office. She needed to be by herself, somewhere she was able to sit and think. Chloe was away from her desk and Kate didn't want to talk to anyone else. Without even announcing her departure, she picked up her coat and bag and made her way outside.

She walked slowly to the coffee shop where she'd met Geraint Winner. Mindful of what had happened last time she'd had a 'real' coffee, Kate played it safe with herbal tea. The café was quiet and warm, and some pleasant folk-type music was playing, a young girl's voice sweetly soaring over violin and piano. Kate sat back on of the deep leather armchairs with a sigh of satisfaction.

She drew out her notebook. Right. Mark Gregory. She thought back to what – who had it been? Oh yes, Chloe – Chloe had said about the collapse of his alibi. Geraint Winner had told the police he'd seen Gregory near the college on the night of Mae's disappearance, that was right, wasn't it? When she'd first heard that, Kate had to admit she'd been sceptical. She was even sceptical of Geraint's assertation that he'd been moved to tell the truth about Mae and her tutor after seeing her parents' heartfelt plea for information on television. But if Gregory *himself* had now admitted that he had been near the quarry and the college on the night Mae disappeared, then it appeared that that was actually the case.

Why had he kept quiet? To Kate, that was obvious – like most men and women having an affair, they didn't want to get caught. They wanted to have their cake and eat it. Then again... Kate took a sip of her drink, rather nice actually, with notes of lemon and rosehips. She'd worked enough cases to know that infidelity and its repercussions could have the most devastating effects. People had killed to silence their affair partners. Affair partners had killed their lover's wives or husbands. It wasn't beyond the realms of possibility that Mae had threatened to tell Gregory's wife if he – what? Wouldn't leave her for Mae?

But *if* – and it was a big *if* – if Gregory had killed Mae, where was the body? The woods and surrounding areas of the college and the quarry had been searched, right down to the very blades of grass.

Taking another sip of tea, Kate looked away from her notes for a moment. There was a local paper on the table in front of her and she scanned the headlines almost automatically. Mae's name was nowhere to be seen; she was old news now, Kate thought with sadness. Although given the arrest of Mark Gregory, not for long... She picked up the paper to look more closely, wondering if she would see Tin's by-line on there. There was nothing very exciting, merely a mention of a royal visit by the King to a new hospital in Wallingham and a smaller headline about an art fraud case over in Bristol.

Kate took a last sip of cooling tea and re-read that particular article. Then she frowned and reached for her phone.

Chapter Twenty-Seven

"Have you heard of Roadster?"

"Who?" Anderton's one word response gave Kate an immediate answer.

"That's what I thought."

Anderton glanced at her as they drove towards the registry office. "You're saying that like I should know who that is. Or what it is."

"No, I don't. Don't worry about it for now, it's not important." Anderton was still glancing over at her in concern and Kate laughed. "Look, watch the road. Let's go for lunch afterwards and I'll tell you about it."

"Is it something to do with work?"

"Kind of. Anyway, we're here now." Kate sighed. "Let's get this over with first."

"I sincerely hope you won't be saying that when we're actually here getting married," Anderton remarked as he parked the car in the tiny carpark beyond the registry office building.

The building itself was a small Georgian townhouse, once residential but long since converted into council offices. The exterior kept the symmetrical façade associated with that period of architecture, along with the perfectly proportioned windows and the central doorway. The golden stone had been cleaned and the metal railings that edged the pavement were freshly painted, pointing black tips like spears skywards.

Pleased already, Kate hugged Anderton's arm to her side as they entered the foyer. There was a graceful sweep of staircase that led to the upper floors and, high above them, a glass cupola that let in streams of sunlight. Around the iron frame that held up the glasswork, white plasterwork showed delicate floral motifs and intricate detailing, visible even from the foyer floor twenty feet below.

"Hope the weather's like this on the actual day," Kate murmured as they were led into an office by a smiling, white-haired lady in a navy uniform. Anderton made a noise of agreement.

When they were taken into the room used for most of the ceremonies performed here, Kate found it hard to suppress a cry of delight. The room was circular in shape, filled with natural light from the tall windows that flanked the ornate fireplace at the end of the room.

"The registrar stands here," said the lady – *I'm Pam, I'm the administrator here* – and the couple either side, here and here." She cast a doubtful eye over Kate's shape. "But you obviously can change it around to suit you. You might want to be seated for the ceremony, for example."

"I'm sure I'll manage," said Kate, biting back a giggle. She took another look around the room. Antique-style chairs were arranged in a semi-circle, facing the fireplace and two truly magnificent floral displays spilled from silver vases on either end of the mantlepiece. Kate remarked as much to Pam.

"Oh, I'm afraid we don't supply those, dear, they're left over from a ceremony we had yesterday. Lovely, aren't they? But you'd be welcome to bring your own."

"Of course." Kate looked around the room once more. Despite her agreement with Anderton that they'd just have two witnesses, she felt a momentary qualm. Should they invite more?

Anderton appeared to read her mind. "Don't forget, Kate, we're having a party afterwards. This is just the official bit."

"Oh, yes, the reception," twittered Pam. "Let me show you to the drawing room downstairs, we do offer a package there which you might be interested in."

Having seen the drawing room – wood-panelled, elegant, an enormous chandelier twinkling above the marble floor – and decided, as one, that it was way too fancy for either of them, Anderton and Kate signed the paperwork they needed to and made their way back to the car. Kate felt rather giggly.

"I almost felt like we should bow when we left,"

she said to Anderton, as she got into the passenger seat.

"I know what you mean. It's nice though, isn't it, for the ceremony, I mean?"

Kate squeezed his arm. "Yes, it's lovely."

"Do you have a dress yet?"

"God, you sound like Chloe. No, I don't. I don't even know if I'm going to fit into anything I buy now in the next four weeks, so..."

Anderton grinned. "Well, at least we've got the ball rolling. Now... lunch?"

The registry office was near the Green Man pub. They settled themselves there in a window seat, wanting to make the most of the spring sunshine, and ordered.

"What was it you were going to tell me about?" asked Anderton.

Kate, sipping her lemonade, had forgotten. "What?"

"You asked me if I'd heard of something. Something about a road?"

"Oh yes. Roadster." Kate put down her lemonade glass. "He – or possibly she – or even they – are a kind of guerrilla artist. You know, like Banksy, that kind of thing."

"Oh Lord, like who?"

Kate rolled her eyes. "Come on, even you've heard of Banksy."

"Isn't he the one who sold a painting for millions and then chopped it up, or something like that?"

"That's the one. Anyway, Roadster's our local equivalent. Listen..." Kate tapped her phone screen and read out loud. "Their work often features provocative social themes and political commentary, often using simplistic imagery to convey complex messages."

Anderton gave her a look. "And?"

Kate grinned. "Well, I only read that bit out because of wanting to sound intellectual. But I saw this—" She produced the newspaper she'd purloined from the coffee shop and showed him the front page. "It made me think, what if the gallery in Salterton is up to something like, I don't know, faking Roadster art?"

Anderton took the page from her and perused it. "Hmm. Is his or hers or their work *that* lucrative?"

"It seems to be."

"And where's your evidence that this gallery is faking anything, Kate?"

"Ah." Kate sagged a little. "That's where I run into a bit of a dead end. It's just – the owner, this really rather dodgy guy called Finian Hobbsley – he was so reluctant to show me the current projects he's working on."

"So?"

"So, it wasn't until he asked me whether I knew anything about art and I said that I didn't, that he was willing to show me."

"And?"

"Well, I managed to get a snap of his current picture, when he was out of the room getting me some water." Kate smiled, patting her stomach. "May as well play the pregnancy card, when I can, huh?"

Anderton shook his head. "You're not convincing me, darling."

Kate held out her phone again. "Doesn't that look a bit like a Roadster work?"

With a look of deep distrust, Anderton took her phone and looked at the picture she'd brought up on screen. Kate, affecting nonchalance as she ate her meal, watched him out of the corner of her eye.

After a lengthy perusal, Anderton put down the phone. "I couldn't possibly comment. Honestly, Kate, you know I respect your intuition, you know I think you're a damn good copper but – seriously love – in this case, I think you're clutching at straws."

He gave her a half smile across the table. Kate, saying nothing, picked up her phone and looked once more at the picture she'd snapped. Looking at it again, now, with Anderton's clear-eyed analysis ringing in her ears, she saw – or rather *didn't* see – what he meant.

"It's an idea," said Anderton, gently. "And it does sound as though the gallery could do with some further investigation. But this..." He reached out and took Kate's free hand. "This, I'm sorry love. This, in my opinion, is a no-goer."

Kate put down the phone with a sigh. She hadn't eaten much but she had now lost her appetite completely and she could feel heartburn beginning to sear the top of her stomach. She reached for her water glass; suddenly sick of work, sick of pregnancy, sick of herself.

"Maybe you're right," she muttered.

"Don't beat yourself up about it," encouraged Anderton. "You've had plenty of ideas which have really moved a case on. You're not God, darling, you're not omniscient."

"I know." Kate tried not to sound as surly as she felt.

"Give yourself a break."

Kate sighed. Perhaps she should. Perhaps it *was* time to take a step back.

"I know," she said, again. "Can we pay, and get out of here?"

Chapter Twenty-Eight

It was the sirens that woke her. Mae, huddled on her slippery gold sofa, heard them in her sleep. She only slept lightly now, constantly on edge for his visits, and the wail of the siren, getting increasingly louder, sounded first in her dream. She had dreamt of the quarry, but not as it had been when she was last there, moving through the night to meet Mark, as they had so often before. Not the quarry that night, when *he* had grabbed her. In Mae's dream, the quarry was golden with sunlight, as it had been for the summer before, when she and Mark had fallen in love. They had been so in love. In the dream, the forest floor of the quarry had been springy with moss and fresh grass, as it had been in real life. In the dream, there had been bird song from the trees. But the bird song had changed, from sweet fluting melody to repetitive robot wailing, a sound remembered from her previous life. A sound of blue and white light. A sound that meant rescue.

Mae gasped and sprang up, instantly awake. The room was dark and no light fell from outside, no light could fall, but she could hear the sirens, she could *hear* them. She scrabbled at the door, feeling her broken nails scratch at the wood. Did she dare scream? Memories of what had happened before when she didn't do as she was told stopped her mouth. She moaned, unable to make a sound louder than that. Would the police hear her anyway, down here (she was sure she was down underground somewhere, somewhere subterranean)? Would *he* hear her?

Sobbing, unable to find it in her to make a sound that might bring rescue or bring harm, Mae collapsed back on her sofa. She could feel the loose edge of the fabric against the skin of her back. He hadn't yet noticed it as she'd tucked it away, but it was useless anyway, she'd not been able to find anything that was sharp enough to use.

The sirens died. If Mae strained her ears, she could hear, very faintly, the murmur of voices. Surely, there would be shouts, rather than murmurs, if the police or whoever it was were here to rescue her? It was that realisation that stopped her once more from screaming, shouting, trying to draw attention to herself.

She waited in the dark for what seemed like hours. The voices faded away. She stayed at her vigil, straining her ears. There was the very faint slam of a door, or so she thought. No more sirens, just the far-off noise of a vehicle engine.

Eventually, weariness and the cold dampness of the floor drove her back to the chaise longue. She arranged herself on it the only way she had found that was remotely comfortable; on her side, with her back tucked against the raised back, where she'd ripped the fabric. She tried to ease the chain around her wrist, thinking that the skin beneath the velvet had at last toughened and stopped chafing. But in a way, that was worse, because it meant she had been here – wherever here was – long enough for that to have happened.

Mae closed her eyes, darkness against the dark. Her heartbeat had returned to normal after the shock of her wakening, and she tried to slow her breathing down so she would go back to sleep. To go back to sleep again and be back in the quarry, in the sunshine and the fresh air – that would be the best thing.

It was just as she was drifting off, with the sound of birdsong in her ears, that she remembered where she'd heard the name Poppy before. *Poppy*. She remembered but, trembling on the edge of unconsciousness, she could not cogitate about the meaning of the word, what it would mean for her. The quarry was there for Mae and she ran towards it, gladly.

Chapter Twenty-Nine

Kate passed a bad night the evening after they'd got back from the pub. Heartburn and indigestion meant she slept badly, and her restlessness was not improved by the twins kicking her for what felt like the whole of the night. She got up the next morning feeling battered and bruised both inside and out.

Anderton had gone out for an early meeting, which Kate was quite glad about as she didn't have to pretend to be okay at the breakfast table. Not that she felt like breakfast. Reluctantly, just because she knew she'd feel worse if she didn't eat at least something, she forced down a slice of buttered toast. *Can't even have a bloody coffee...* Nearly weeping with self-pity, she took a shower, dressed herself in the rapidly dwindling number of clothes that actually fit her and stomped down the stairs to her car. *Sod walking, sod everything.*

Anderton's words of the previous day kept recurring to her. She heard them without anger at him but with plenty at herself. What on earth had she been thinking, coming up with such an outlandish theory? Art fraud? As if that would have anything to do with Mae Denton's disappearance anyway. Kate thanked whichever deity was around that she hadn't mentioned this to anyone at work. Or had she? Her tiredness was exacerbating her memory problems.

Maybe I *should* take maternity leave early, she thought, as she drove to the station. Maybe it is time to take a break. I'm not getting anywhere and I'm not contributing anything except for *stupid* theories that, if I'd spent even five minutes considering them, don't even stack up...

"Don't talk to me," she warned Chloe, the moment she got to her desk. "I'm not in a good mood."

Chloe raised her eyebrows but said nothing other than, "Okay." She was no fool.

Kate turned to her computer in a dark mood. She ran through her emails, disposing of those she could (and to be honest, a couple of those she couldn't) with a ruthless bang of the delete button. She checked her calendar and to-do list and dismissed both with a snort.

God, she needed coffee. A hot drink of something would do but she didn't want to get up and brave the kitchen area because, well, people. To be honest, she didn't want to get *up*. Kate turned her attention back to the computer screen, gritting her teeth.

Work. Who could be bothered... She brought up

Google and typed 's' in the search box, meaning to type the word which currently summed up her view of the world. Her previous searches appeared in the drop-down list. At the top was Sea Views, which brought a little extra kick of humiliation to the day.

Kate, sighing loudly enough for Chloe to raise her eyebrows once more (although the sensible woman kept her mouth shut), clicked on the link in a masochistic kind of way. She looked at the various pages and eventually onto the biography page of Finian Hobbsley, which she'd read before but some time ago. Listlessly, her eyes ran down the list of his accomplishments until it reached one of the last sentences. *Before founding Sea Views, Finian Hobbsley worked at Granello Fine Arts until its closure in 20--.*

Kate blinked. She read the sentence again. What was it that was tugging at her memory? She knew something about those words was familiar... She read it once more. Of course, Granello Fine Arts.

That had been an art gallery in Abbeyford, hadn't it? Kate sat back, the back of her office chair creaking as she leant against it. Granello Fine Arts. Now in what context had she heard that name?

Still thinking, she pushed herself out of her chair and made her way to the kitchenette. Something about that art gallery name was nagging at her. She'd heard it connected with a case before, but when? Once more, Kate cursed her memory.

"You buggers have a lot to answer for," she muttered to the twins as she poured hot water onto a cranberry and raspberry teabag.

"What's that?" Martin appeared at her elbow, holding an empty mug in his hand.

Kate smiled, a little embarrassed. "Oh, nothing."

He smiled in return, in his rather reserved way and reached for the coffee jar. Kate, not wanting to get into conversation (although with Martin, that was never a given anyway) turned to go. Then she turned back.

"Martin, does Granello Fine Arts mean anything to you?"

Theo, for example, would have reared his head back in overdone surprise and said something sarcastic, and probably called her 'woman' for good measure. Martin gave her words his quiet attention for a full thirty seconds before he nodded.

"Yes, that's the art gallery that was in Abbeyford, wasn't it? The one who's owner – co-owner, wasn't he? Anyway, he had that funny head in a jar. It was when those feet were found."

How could Kate have forgotten? "Oh Martin, of course. How could I have forgotten? The feet!"

Martin smiled. "Well, I remember because that was my very first case here."

"Of course it was." Kate had forgotten that too. "Yes, the feet. Gosh, that's a while ago now, isn't it?"

"A few years, yes."

"The head in the jar... yes. I remember. The owner

died from AIDS, didn't he?" Kate was thinking aloud now. "No, that was the other one. The one who owned the gallery. Not the first one—" She became aware that she was babbling a little. "Anyway, it doesn't matter. Thanks Martin."

"It's no problem."

Kate took her mug back to her desk, shaking her head at her memories of that case, now flooding back. Granello Fine Arts – yes, they had been co-owners, the owner of the gallery and the other man, the one with the head in the jar, an old film prop that a burglar had mistaken for an actual human head. Kate laughed out loud at the memory, causing Chloe to look up.

"Can I talk to you now?"

Kate, laughter subsiding but still with a smile on her face, nodded. "Yes. Sorry."

Chloe blew out her cheeks. "You looked in a proper fouler when you got in."

"I was. Sorry."

"What's so funny?"

Kate told her, reminding her of the case. "Do you remember?"

"Of course I do. He – the guy with the head- what was his name? He had that amazing house out on Park Lane. Unbelievable."

"That's right. Oh yes, that was lovely." Kate thought back to it, a mansion really, stuffed with sculptures, artwork and beautiful, tasteful things.

"What's brought that up?"

"Well, it's funny." Kate gave Chloe a quick rundown of what had happened. "It's probably nothing but it might be worth having a word with that guy, the co-owner of Granello. If he's even here in Abbeyford still."

Chloe gave her a cynical look. "Hey, if you had a house like that, would you ever want to move?"

Kate shrugged. "People do. Didn't he live there with his mother?"

"Yeah. Yeah, he did. She was very elderly, wasn't she?"

"Yes. Gosh, it's a while ago. I don't really remember." Kate laughed again, this time at herself. "I don't remember anything at the moment."

"What's my name?"

"Bird, isn't it?" Kate gave Chloe a grin. "Anyway, I'll pop over and see that guy and see if he can tell me anything more about Finian Hobbsley. Or his bloody gallery."

"Good plan."

Kate heaved herself up again to try and find the file for the old case. The storeroom where the paperwork was kept was always chilly, and today was no exception. She prayed that the file wouldn't be one of the storage cabinets on floor level, as she wasn't sure she'd be able to get down that far to reach it. Or more pertinently, if she got down that far, that she'd be able to get back up.

As it turned out, the documentation was easily

reached, over in the far corner of the large room. Kate took it back to the desk to have a read-through. Chloe had taken herself off for an early lunch, so Kate was able to read through the casefiles without interruption. Her earlier tiredness had dissipated. Possibly camomile tea was of some use after all? Kate made herself another, just in case it was.

Terence Buchanan, *that* was the man's name, the one with the house on Park Lane. Kate could remember him, now she had the data in front of her. Quite a distinguished looking man, if she remembered correctly; dark glasses and about forty-five, possibly older. His mother was – Kate took another look at the file – Mary Warner, a tiny, very elderly lady, left a rich widow by her husband.

Her thoughts were interrupted by movement across the office. She looked up to see that Olbeck had come back to his office. Before he could be trapped on one of the innumerable calls he took and made every day, Kate panted across the room to speak to him.

"How's it going with Gregory?"

Olbeck looked tired. He was one of those men who had to shave daily, and stubble was already showing in a bluish film along his jawbone. He rubbed his head distractedly as he waved Kate to a seat.

"Had to release him. We haven't got anything yet to make a charge stick."

"What have you got?"

Olbeck sank into his chair with an air of resignation. "Nothing but his own admission that he was going to meet Mae at the quarry that evening."

"And – it's not enough?" Kate knew it wasn't.

"No, it's not. We've got a warrant for his place though, hopefully that'll bring up something."

"That's good—" Kate began before a cramp zipped across her belly, bringing a gasp to her lips.

"What's wrong? Are you okay?"

Kate held her breath. The cramp intensified and then ebbed away. She waited to see if there would be another.

"Are you okay?" Olbeck sounded more worried.

Kate breathed out slowly. "I'm – okay. I think. Just got a bit of a pain."

Olbeck looked at her closely. "You don't look great, to be honest."

"Oh, thanks—"

He gave her a wry look. "I mean it. Honestly, why don't you head home and rest for a bit? There's nothing much going on here that you need to concern yourself with."

Kate was about to tell him about the Granello link with Finian Hobbsley, but a second pain drove it from her mind. This time the pain was fainter, but it was enough to make her uneasy.

"Yes, yes, you're right. I'll go home."

"Good. And make sure you *rest*."

"I will. Promise."

Chapter Thirty

It was over a day before he came with food. Mae knew this because of the cycle of her hunger; the gradual swelling of it, stomach rumbling louder and louder, the nausea and the dizziness. The slow fade of hunger after she could do nothing to assuage it. She had to pee in one corner of the room, unable to hold on any longer, and hoped to God that she wouldn't be beaten for it.

She didn't allow herself to think of whether he wouldn't come at all. One glimpse of a truncated future in which that possibility happened meant that she would die. She would die like a trapped animal in a cage.

That's exactly what I am. Mae, lying on her chaise-longue, eyed the pool of urine in the corner, the black and white floor tiles beneath it. She remembered a long-ago lesson from school about explorers in the Australian desert, how they'd drunk their own urine in a mostly futile attempt to not die of dehydration. Could she do that?

I could. I think I could. As time went by, Mae knew

that she was going to have to contemplate behaviour that a free Mae would never have countenanced. This was different, this was survival. She didn't have the luxury of morality.

She had heard no more sirens, no more voices. She had heard nothing. Had those sirens been, perhaps, an ambulance? Had he been taken to hospital? If something had happened to him, something that meant he would be in hospital for some time, then she would die. If he had died, she would die.

Don't think about that. Mae tried to turn her thoughts to the quarry, to the sunshine, but it was impossible. She slowed her breathing, closing her eyes and trying to get comfortable on her slippery perch.

She must have dozed for a bit because the sound of his footsteps outside and the rattle of keys in the door jerked her awake. She cast a glance towards the puddle of urine which had shrunk a little and braced herself as he came into the room.

He looked awful. That was her first thought. Behind his glasses, his eyes were red-rimmed, sore-looking and glassy. He was normally dressed formally, in an ironed shirt, tie and suit trousers but today he was, incredibly, wearing grey tracksuit trousers and a dirty black jumper.

Mae's heart jumped. She remembered his look at her that last time, as if she'd disappointed him. Not like Poppy, but then nobody was. What had he said? *But then Poppy was a one off.* Poppy Taige, that was who he had been talking about. Mae knew now that's who he meant, had remembered why she knew that name. Poppy, the girl who had disappeared, years ago now.

For a tense moment, they looked at each other. Mae braced herself, thinking he would rush in and beat her again. But instead, he looked at her for another moment and then took something out from behind his back and threw it into the room.

Mae flinched. It was a brown paper bag with the logo of a red rooster on it, grease-stained. It was such a shocking reminder of the outside world, the one she'd left behind, that she couldn't help herself but cry out. He took no notice but stared at her for a moment longer. With disgust, it looked like. Again, Mae braced herself for violence but, after another moment, he turned and locked the door, leaving her alone with a brown takeaway bag on the floor.

Mae expelled her breath. She picked up the bag, flinching for a moment when she wondered what could be in it. But it was alright, she could smell the chicken inside it, fatty and greasy and suddenly the most desirable thing she had ever smelt. Hunger came roaring back.

She opened the bag. There were three bits of chicken in there, coated in orange breadcrumbs. Chicken thighs. Weeping a little, Mae lifted a piece to her mouth. She didn't care if it were poisoned, that it was cold; she attacked it like a starving animal. *I am a starving animal.* Her mouth was full of chicken, and she chewed and swallowed frantically, until her teeth scraped on the bone within the thigh itself.

Mae's chewing slowed. Her tongue explored the bone within the thigh. She drew the chicken from her mouth and looked at it, looked at the ragged bits of flesh surrounding the thigh bone. The hard, dense, thighbone.

Chapter Thirty-One

KATE DROVE HERSELF HOME SLOWLY and carefully. She carried her bump into the house as if balancing a precious vase in her arms. The house was quiet, warm and clean and, despite her worry about the babies, Kate sent up a little prayer of gratitude, that she had such a lovely place to live. The perfect house in which to bring up children.

Please, let me bring up my children. Don't take them from me. She knew she was panicking, she knew she was probably being silly but she couldn't help a breathless murmur as she lay herself down on the sofa. *Please be okay, please be okay.*

She had been lying there for barely ten minutes when she heard Anderton's key in the door and felt a burst of gladness.

"Kate? What are you doing home so early?" Anderton's face contracted as the implications of her early arrival home struck him. "Are you okay? Are the babies okay?"

It was ridiculous but now he was here, Kate found herself thinking she'd panicked herself over nothing.

The pain she'd felt in the office was gone completely and the twins were stirring gently under her hands. Olbeck had been right – she had needed the rest. She told Anderton just that.

"Should I call the hospital? The midwife?"

Kate reached for his hand, wanting to wipe the strain from his face. "I'm okay, honestly. I think I just needed a rest."

"Oh, you worried me." Anderton put his own hand over Kate's, resting on her stomach. "Boy, you worried me."

"I'm okay," Kate said, again. She struggled up to a sitting position.

"Do you think we should just pop to the maternity unit, just in case?"

Kate shook her head. "No, really. I'm really feeling much better."

Anderton looked at her for a long moment once more. Then he nodded. "Well, if you're sure, I'll make us a pot of tea. Decaff, obviously."

"Obviously," said Kate, trying not to sigh. She watched as he left the room, her gaze drifting over the furniture, the wood-burner, the rug in front where Merlin had slept his last sleep. *Dear old cat*.

Anderton came back with a tea-tray, no less, teapot, milk jug and a plate of biscuits. Kate giggled. "I feel a proper invalid now."

"You may jest," said Anderton, pouring her a cup.

"But I've been having a think while the tea was brewing. Can I just come out and say it?"

Kate paused with the cup to her mouth. "Ooh. Now, that sounds serious."

"Well, hear me out."

"Okay, then. Go on."

Anderton looked her in the eye. "I think you should stop work."

There was a silence. Kate sifted through all the feelings his words had invoked in her. Immediate and knee-jerk outrage. Then a pause for reflection. Guilt. Sadness. Excitement. Relief.

Anderton was watching her with some anxiety. "What do you think?"

"I think," Kate said slowly, having put her thoughts in order. "I think you might be right."

Anderton blew out his cheeks with a rush of air. "It's just – I want to see you through to thirty-six weeks, Kate." Thirty-six weeks was the average length of a twin pregnancy, as they both knew from their antenatal classes. "I don't want my babies to spend their first weeks in a neonatal unit."

"Do you think *I* do?" snapped Kate, unable to help herself. Then immediately, seeing the hurt on his face, added, "No, I know. You're right. It's just—"

"I know. I know how important your work is to you, darling."

"Yes."

Anderton offered her the plate of biscuits, but she shook her head. "I mean, you *are* going to have to leave at some point. Probably in the not-too-distant future."

"Yes, I know." Every word he was saying, Kate was agreeing with, but that didn't make it any easier. But then, hadn't she herself thought that it was time for a break, just this morning. Had it *been* this morning? That was the other thing, her memory was beginning to be a liability. There was no point her doing her job if she couldn't actually do it properly.

It still stung though. Kate closed her eyes and breathed deeply. The babies looped within her, as if they were dancing. I can't wait to meet you, she thought. Who are you going to be? What are you going to look like?

"Kate?"

She opened her eyes and smiled at her fiancée. "I'm fine. I agree. I'll talk to Mark tomorrow." There was something that she should do though, before she left – just chase up that lead to Finian Hobbsley, visit what's-his-name, Terence Buchanan. But she didn't need to mention that to Anderton just now, it wasn't that important. She would go tomorrow.

Out loud, she said, "Thank you for the tea."

Kate slept surprisingly well that night. As she made herself toast the next morning, she wondered whether it was because she'd made a firm decision about work, and stopping it. Perhaps it had been preying on her mind more than she had acknowledged. She remembered the anxiety of the early weeks of pregnancy, especially once they'd found out about the twins.

Although she hadn't marked it on the calendar, week twenty-seven had been emblazoned on her brain. The magical week, the week in which if the babies came too soon, they just *might* have a chance of survival.

That week was long gone and although she had never become complacent, perhaps the demands of her work had pushed the anxiety of a miscarriage or stillbirth a little further back in her mind. But – as she imagined it was for every expectant mother – it was always there.

If the twins were born now, they would almost certainly survive. But it was still too early, way too early for comfort. Kate swallowed the last piece of toast, with difficulty, as she had a lump in her throat. That was the other thing as well, she was so *emotional* now and in a job like hers, that was not a good thing. Of course you had to *care*, of course you had to empathise, but a degree of detachment was needed, for you to be able to do your work properly. Like a surgeon, thought Kate and snorted laughter at her delusions of grandeur.

Dear, oh dear. Up one minute, down the next... hormones were the very devil. Shaking her head at herself, she put her mug and plate in the dishwasher and went for her shower. She'd pop in on Terence Buchanan on the way to work, get the lowdown (if there was any) on Finian Hobbsley and then head to work, to hand in her notice for maternity leave.

Chapter Thirty-Two

Rain was freckling the windscreen as Kate drove off from her house, but as she joined the main round, it increased to a downpour, sheets of water falling from the sky. It was warm though – warm in terms of how frigid it had been over the past months. Good for the garden, Kate thought, trying to be optimistic as she peered through the windscreen wipers battling the torrent.

She was feeling quite sanguine about her decision to stop work, surprising herself. Work had been her life for so long, she would have thought that she would be feeling a bit more conflicted about giving it up, more than a bit anxious and worried about the future. But she didn't feel like that at all. *It's time. I'm ready for my new life.*

Of course, there was no question of her giving up the police *entirely*. That was something that she and Anderton hadn't even had to discuss. Kate knew, babies or no babies, that she would be returning to work at some point. But at what that point was, she had little idea. One day at a time, through pregnancy and through life, that was her motto.

She vaguely remembered the way to Park Lane and didn't even bother to turn on the satnav. She drove along the road that led to the turning, remembering coming here with Chloe, those years ago. It had been a beautiful spring day then, hadn't it? Kate tried to remember. Hadn't that been when Chloe and Roman had started dating? Poor Roman. Kate paused in her thoughts to remember him fleetingly and give thanks for Chloe's happier life nowadays.

Here it was, the turning to Park Lane. A wide private road, with just a few, enormous houses. A quiet street that led into woodland at the end of the road. When Kate parked the car and got out, all she could hear was birdsong, not even the traffic noise from the road penetrating this far down the lane.

She hadn't rung ahead and thought it was very possible that Terence Buchanan wouldn't be in, although it was more likely his mother would be. If Kate remembered correctly, Mary Warner walked with a stick and was almost infirm. Kate puffed her way up the flight of stone steps that led to the front door of the enormous house, and knocked.

The brass doorknocker was gigantic, shaped like an upended horseshoe. Hadn't Martin told her once that horseshoes were hung like that to stop the luck spilling out? Or was it the other way that was lucky, as then the devil couldn't sit within the curve?

And did it actually matter? Kate laughed at the nonsense her mind came up with and brought herself back to the presence. Nobody had answered her knock, so she tried again.

After a wait of two minutes, there was still no answer. Even the old lady must be out. Sighing, Kate turned to go.

Then she stopped.

Out of nowhere, a wave of fear came over her, no, not fear, but something unpleasant – anxiety, anger, a sense of impending doom. It was so strong that she almost cried out – she spun back to face the door, expecting to see something there that would account for her sudden distress – but there was nothing – merely the closed door, just as it had been.

Kate paused. She was actually sweating, she was surprised to find; sweating and her fingers were shaking. Something was wrong, she could feel it – at some subconscious level, some subterranean feeling was making itself known to her.

Was it the babies? She thought of the pain she'd gone through yesterday. Oh god, oh god, what if something was really wrong with the babies and she hadn't heeded it? Was her body trying to tell her something, was it trying to warn her?

Almost on the edge of her hearing, Kate heard something then, a moan, or a shout, or something other than that. An animal noise, something hurt. Coming from where, from inside the house? Heart thumping, Kate turned back once more to the door. She saw her fingers go up to the doorknocker once more and then stop, moving themselves to the wood of the door itself and pushing.

What was she thinking? Just as she was telling herself not to be so ridiculous, the door would not be open, it moved backwards from her pushing hand, clicking open. It must have been resting on the latch, as these old doors often did. It opened slowly, silently, revealing an empty hallway that Kate vaguely remembered from her visit here before. The same polished floorboards, the paintings and artwork on the walls, a small chandelier like a waterfall of diamonds hanging from the high ceiling.

Kate paused. She could feel her heart thudding away at her ribs. She felt as if she were being pulled in two; one half of her, the police officer half, knew that she had to go into this house, find that noise, see what was so badly wrong. The pregnant half of her screamed internally, are you crazy? Don't put yourself in danger, call someone, do *not* go in there...

But she was still an officer, more so perhaps than she was a mother, yet. Kate edged her way into the hallway, air moving against the sweat on her face. The sound came again, a low moan from deep in the house.

This was stupid, this was reckless. She didn't even have a weapon. Thinking this all the while, Kate crept forward, straining her ears, holding herself ready to run. Run, what was she thinking, she wouldn't be able to run...

The hallway turned at the end into another corridor, which led to another corridor. At the back of that corridor was a door, half open, darkness beyond it. The sound was coming from there. It sounded like an animal, a badly wounded animal.

As if propelled by something she couldn't resist, Kate moved forward. As she got closer to the doorway, she could see stairs beyond it, stone stairs, leading downwards. To the cellar, perhaps, or a floor below the house... Swallowing, she edged forward a little. Within her, one twin kicked at the tension on her body.

Kate, trying not to make a sound, found her keys and the little torch she always kept on her keyring. The torch beam made a thin, white light in the darkness. Kate stood at the top of the stairs, snatching a glance behind her to see that nobody had crept up on her. As spooked as she was, she could tell that there was no one in the rooms behind her; the ground floor had an empty feel to it, she could just tell.

Do I go down there? Every fibre of her being was screaming at her not to. But then came a sound recognisable as a human word, a word spoken, sobbed by a child or a young girl. *Oh no, oh no.*

Without thinking, Kate propelled herself down the stairs, moving as fast as she could. The torch beam strobed and jittered over the damp stone of the walls surrounding the staircase. How deep were these stairs? Kate guessed that she was fully underground now, the daylight from the top of the stairs fading fast as she descended.

At the bottom of the stairs was a door and beyond that, another door, a door that you would expect to see in a correctional facility or perhaps a mental hospital, a door bristling with bolts and locks. This stood open and beyond was bright light, spilling out into the darkness.

Oh, no. Oh, no.

Kate held her breath. She stepped through the first doorway and pushed open the heavy, metal edged door, revealing what was beyond. Her held breath exploded out in shock when she saw what was there.

The body of a man lay on the floor, surrounded by a lake of blood, glossy and scarlet against the black and white tiles of the floor. Spotlights burned down from the high ceiling, illuminating the carnage below as if highlighting a particularly dramatic moment in a play. Beyond the dead man sat a girl, an emaciated, wide-eyed girl, one hand clamped in a metal handcuff which was clamped itself to a long chain. The girl's dirty hair fell over her face as she rocked and moaned, her free hand holding something small and whitish-brown and blood-smeared.

Kate and Mae looked at each other. Kate knew she should call for help, knew she should preserve the scene but at that moment, all she did was hold out her arms and Mae, sobbing and shaking, got up from the grubby gold chaise longue she'd been sitting on and threw herself into them.

Chapter Thirty-Three

"She stabbed him with a *chicken bone*?"

Kate, resting her head against the back of her chair with her eyes closed, nodded.

"Christ." She opened them to see Theo holding his hands to his head. "Now I've heard everything. I mean, like, *seriously*, I've heard everything."

Kate felt too exhausted to say anything in response, so merely made a 'hmm' sound, which Theo could interpret any way he wanted.

"So, he's definitely dead?"

Chloe sprang forward with a protective arm. "Give it a rest, Theo, can't you? Can't you see she's done in?"

"Sorry." Theo dropped down into a handy chair, churning his hair. "It's just, though – *Christ*. You know?"

Kate made an effort. "I know."

Both Chloe and Theo were looking at her with concern. "Are you sure you should be here, bird?" asked Chloe. "I can update you later if it's just the debrief you're staying for?"

"It's fine." Kate didn't want to add the sentence

that was in her mind. *It's probably the last time I'm going to be here in the office for a while.* She really didn't have the energy to deal with the consequences of uttering *that* thought aloud.

At that moment, Olbeck entered the office. He looked tired but relieved, a state of mind that Kate thought was echoed in all of her fellow officers.

"Gather round, people, gather round." He caught sight of Kate and frowned. "Kate, I really think you ought to go home. It's been a shock to you, if nothing else."

"I'm okay," said Kate, trying to keep her eyes open.

Olbeck gave her a dubious glance. "Well – if you're sure..."

"I'm okay," said Kate, repeating herself once more. "But afterwards, could I have a quick word?"

"Sure, sure." She suspected he was barely listening, although given the events of the day, that was hardly surprising.

Olbeck cleared his throat. "Right. As I'm sure you're aware, Mae Denton had been found alive – I don't necessarily say well, but she's alive and from the first examination at hospital, she appears to be physically unharmed. She's lost weight and obviously the psychological effects of the trauma will be—" He paused, as if weighing up his words. "Well, we all know the kind of thing that could happen."

There was a moment's silence. Kate felt once again the slight weight of the girl's body in her arms, the sharp angles of her shoulder blades beneath Kate's palms. *Poor girl.*

Olbeck continued. "Terence Buchanan, the owner of the house in which Mae was found, is dead. He was found – by Kate, thank you, Kate – stabbed through the neck with a sharp object—"

"A bloody chicken bone," interjected Theo, still in tones of disbelief.

"Yes, a chicken bone. She sharpened it with her teeth." Olbeck looked as disbelieving as Theo for a moment. "It seems incredible, yes, but she was desperate, fighting for her life. Mae hasn't actually said anything about killing him, but we all know it's obvious that she stabbed him. Apparently he'd been keeping her prisoner for weeks, ever since she disappeared. He abducted her from the quarry that night and has held her in the cellar of his house ever since."

"All that time," said Chloe, shaking her head.

"Mae told Kate that she'd heard sirens one night. We've checked and an ambulance was despatched to Park Lane a few days ago, to attend Mary Warner, Buchanan's mother, who'd had a fall." The room waited. Olbeck went on. "Mary Warner died in hospital that same night."

Kate spoke up. "Mae thought that's why he'd given her the chicken. He couldn't be bothered with anything more elaborate. Normally he wouldn't give her food like that."

He wanted me to be pure. I had to be pure. She could hear the girl's voice in her head right now.

Rav spoke up, rather unwisely in Kate's opinion. "What about Mark Gregory?"

Olbeck grimaced. "Well, we released him yesterday, anyway. He may not be best pleased with us, but we were following procedure. There'll be no cause for complaint."

Theo was nodding. "He'd better not bloody try."

Kate thought of all the repercussions, now that Mae was safe. The affair, the friendships, Mae's family – everyone involved would be affected by the revelations of Mae's secrets. But perhaps they would all be so pleased and relieved to have her back that something positive might come out of it all? Kate didn't know, but she crossed her fingers for them all.

And for Mae herself? Kate wished, quite passionately, that she would be all right. She had no fears for her in a legal sense – if any case could be shown to be a case of self-defence, she was pretty sure this one would be right up there at the top – but Kate knew herself only too well the long-ranging effects of trauma, how the damage could follow you around for years, lurking in the background, or up in your face. *I hope she'll be okay.*

Olbeck paused and took a sip of water from the glass on the table by his side. "This is something that you may not know." He paused again, looking around at all of them. Something about his expression chilled Kate's blood.

"Human remains have been found at the house. More than one person."

Kate heard a faint gasp from someone, she wasn't sure who. Although she had not known that exact fact, the words that Mae had whispered to her as she rode with her to the hospital had given her a clue. Mae had clung to her so hard that Kate could not have left her alone.

Poppy, Poppy Taige, he took her, he has her, I don't know where...

Shaking herself back to the present, she listened to Olbeck.

"So, as you can all appreciate, this has now become a *much* bigger murder investigation. Forensics are at the scene now and we'll know more shortly, but for now, all leave is cancelled, and we'll be pulling in some people from Salterton as necessary."

Rav spoke up. "Do we have an ID on the remains found yet?"

"I don't know for certain, but I think one of them is Poppy Taige." Kate found herself speaking up without realising she was going to do so.

"Poppy Taige?" Martin had actually gone pale. Kate remembered he'd worked the case in Bristol before transferring here. "Oh my god, that's awful." He sounded so distressed that everyone looked at him in consternation. Martin wasn't usually that emotional. He seemed to realise this. "Sorry, it's just—"

"I know," said Olbeck. "It's awful. But we need to pull together to see this through to the end. *If* those remains are of Poppy Taige and the other missing girls, we can at least bring some sort of closure to their families."

Kate, weariness building within her, thought about seeing Tin's headline in the paper, weeks ago now and feeling like a lifetime ago. *Local Police Baffled by Mystery of Missing Girls.* The words had stung because there was a grain of truth within them. Poppy, Saskia, Hannah, Prisha. Those poor girls, those lost girls... at least now perhaps they could bring them home to their loved ones.

Home. Kate knew, right at that moment, that there was where she and the babies needed to be. The room around her pulsed with energy, people talking, suggesting, Olbeck assigning tasks, phones being snatched up, conversations beginning. But for the babies, she would be right in there with them, but she was so, so weary...

"Kate?"

Her eyes flew open to see Olbeck standing in front of her, half smiling. "Oh. Hello."

"Hello, you. Come into my office."

Kate nodded. She gathered her strength and got up, following her boss and best friend into his office.

"Take a seat."

Kate remained standing. "Honestly, if I sit I down now, I won't get up again."

Olbeck looked at her closely. "I told you to go home."

"Yes."

Kate wanted to say so much more, to thank him for never letting her down, as a friend and as a boss. She wanted to say how much she'd loved working here and how much she loved her colleagues, how she would miss them and miss him. But it was too much to put into words, far too much. She smiled at him.

Olbeck put his head on one side. "You're going to tell me you're leaving. Aren't you?"

"Yes." Again, Kate wanted to say more but this time she couldn't, past the lump in her throat.

Olbeck said nothing. He got up and walked around his desk and put his arms about her. They stood embraced for a moment and then he released her.

"I think that's the right decision," he said. He had tears in his eyes too.

Kate blinked, smiling through her watery vision. "It's not for ever."

"No, it damn well isn't." He put his hands back on her shoulders for a moment, squeezed, and dropped his arms to his sides. "It isn't."

"No."

Olbeck smiled at her. "Go on, then, darling. You head home."

Kate smiled back. "I will."

"Do you want to say goodbye to everyone?"

Kate shook her head. "Not now. It's not the right time, for them or for me."

"Right you are."

Kate gave him one last nod and turned away. With her hand on the doorhandle, she turned back. "Besides, it won't be goodbye. It'll be *au revoir*."

Olbeck laughed. "Yes, that exactly."

"Talk soon."

"Talk soon."

Kate smiled and walked out of the room, shutting the office door behind her.

THE END

Enjoyed this book?

An honest review left at your favourite retailer and Goodreads is always welcome, and really important for indie authors, helping us with our marketing and promotion, and finding us new readers. Thank you in advance.

Want some more of Celina Grace's work for free?

Subscribers to her mailing list get a free digital copy of Requiem (A Kate Redman Mystery: Book 2) and a free digital copy of her historical mystery novella Death at the Manor (The Asharton Manor Mysteries: Book 1).

Just got to Celina's website to sign up. It's quick, easy and free! Be the first to be informed of promotions, giveaways, new releases and subscriber-only benefits by signing up to her (occasional) newsletter.

Aspiring or new authors might like to check out Celina's online courses at Academy for Authors, for motivation, inspiration and advice on writing fiction. Get a free eBook and other helpful downloads when you sign up for the newsletter.

celinagracebooks.com
celinagrace.com
academyforauthors.com
Twitter: @celina__grace
Facebook: authorcelinagrace
Instagram: academyforauthors

Requiem
(A Kate Redman Mystery: Book 2)

When the body of troubled teenager Elodie Duncan is pulled from the river in Abbeyford, the case is at first assumed to be a straightforward suicide. Detective Sergeant Kate Redman is shocked to discover that she'd met the victim the night before her death, introduced by Kate's younger brother Jay. As the case develops, it becomes clear that Elodie was murdered. A talented young musician, Elodie had been keeping some strange company and was hiding her own dark secrets.

As the list of suspects begin to grow, so do the questions. What is the significance of the painting Elodie modelled for? Who is the man who was seen with her on the night of her death? Is there any connection with another student's death at the exclusive musical college that Elodie attended?

As Kate and her partner Detective Sergeant Mark Olbeck attempt to unravel the mystery, the dark undercurrents of the case threaten those whom Kate holds most dear...

Death at the Manor
(The Asharton Manor Mysteries: Book 1)
A Novella

It is 1929. Asharton Manor stands alone in the middle of a pine forest, once the place where ancient pagan ceremonies were undertaken in honour of the goddess Astarte. The Manor is one of the most beautiful stately homes in the West Country and seems like a palace to Joan Hart, newly arrived from London to take up a servant's position as the head kitchen maid. Getting to grips with her new role and with her fellow workers, Joan is kept busy, but not too busy to notice that the glittering surface of life at the Manor might be hiding some dark secrets. The beautiful and wealthy mistress of the house, Delphine Denford, keeps falling ill but why? Confiding her thoughts to her friend and fellow housemaid, feisty Verity Hunter, Joan is unsure of what exactly is making her uneasy, but then Delphine Denford dies...

Armed only with their own good sense and quick thinking, Joan and Verity must pit their wits against a cunning murderer in order to bring them to justice.

Acknowledgements

Many thanks to all the following splendid souls:

Chris Howard for his brilliant cover designs; Glendon and the Streetlight Graphics team for formatting; my superb reader team; lifelong friends and Schlockers Ben Robinson and Alberto Lopez, and my heavenly friend David Hall; Ross McConnell, Lindsay McDonnell, Kathy and Pat McConnell, Anthony Alcock, Naomi White, Mo Argyle, Cheryl Beckles, Loletha Stoute, Helen Dear, Helen Watson, Emily Way, Sandy Hall, Kristyna Vosecka, Izzy Siu, Rajini Oliver and of course, my fantastic Jethro and Isaiah.

Printed in Great Britain
by Amazon